The Boy and The Clock Book

The Boy and The Clock Book

■ ■ ■

A. Lynn Bassett

ISBN: 1543022529
ISBN 13: 9781543022520
Library of Congress Control Number: 2016921347
CreateSpace Independent Publishing Platform
North Charleston, South Carolina

1

Charlie's Surprise

Tick-tock, tick-tock. Only three minutes stood between Charlie Higgins and the best summer ever! It was Charlie's last day of school as he sat staring at the clock in Mr. Orangelo's geography class. His teacher knew more about Michigan than anyone in the whole state! He loved school, but something about 7th hour made time stand still, and not in a good way. Maybe it was because of Mr. Orangelo's monotone voice, or perhaps it was the funky smell that came from the locked back corner closet. Either way, it was the last day of sixth grade with only three minutes to go, and Charlie could not wait to get out of there! All the other students had finished their end-of-the-year exams and were silently waiting for the bell to ring. One kid was asleep again at his desk and had managed to cover a good portion of it in drool. Another spent the previous ten minutes seeing how many No. 2 pencils he could balance on the bridge of his nose. And Charlie with his chin resting in his hands, watched as the minute hand slowly ticked closer to two-thirty. Now one minute stood between him and the best summer ever!

Charlie was your basic sixth-grade boy. Shorter than most of the girls, he spent hours playing video games with his friends. He found school, for the most part interesting, except of course for Mr. Orangelo's geography class.

Charlie was fair skinned with freckles (which he hated) and had light brown hair—all traits he inherited from his mother's family in England. For the past week, Charlie and his best friend Ben had been making plans for all the things they were going to do that summer. This was the summer Charlie would finally turn 13, and for the Higgins family, the 13th birthday was a big celebration. Charlie's family cherished the year a boy went from a child to a teenager, and with it came great responsibility. Charlie would have to take on more chores around the house and study extra hard in school to keep his grades up, but there were rewards, too. He would be able to stay up later, contribute to family decisions, and (his favorite) ride his bike downtown with his friends!

At last, the bell rang! Charlie jumped up from his desk, skidded past Mr. Orangelo quickly saying, "Have a good summer," and headed straight for the flag pole. All his friends were waiting there. Some of his buddies lived too far away to see on a regular basis, others were leaving all summer on family vacations or to summer camps, but most of his crew, on Lake Street, would be staying home. Today was the start of the best summer ever! When a twelve-year-old boy has beach volleyball at Thompson Lake, neighborhood basketball tournaments, riding downtown to get ice cream cones from Kelly's Uptown Creamery, skateboarding at the skate park, and hanging out with his pales whenever possible, nothing can spoil his summer!

Charlie signed a few last yearbooks of his friends and said goodbye before heading home. Now, most boys Charlie's age would find their hometowns boring, but not Charlie Higgins. For him, Howell was a place of endless adventure and awesome festivals that he would finally be able to go to alone with his friends! Howell was a great place for a young man to grow up.

Charlie had been walking for a few minutes as he passed by the library. He waved to some classmates as they walked up the library stairs. *Probably going to use the computers*, Charlie thought. But for Charlie, a sunny day like this was wasted glued to a screen. Soon he found himself walking into smelling distance of Guy's Bakery. This place was known for its garlic twist breadsticks which could grab your nose from a block away with its tantalizing garlic aroma! Remembering he had a few bucks in his pocket, Charlie raced to the bakery nearly running over a woman and her miniature poodle. "Sorry!" He exclaimed as he ran past her. *Mom won't mind me buying a few because dinner is not till six,* he convinced himself. As usual there was a line out the door, but he never minded standing in line because he got to smell the garlic twists and watch the bakers make them. By the time Charlie got to the front of the line to order his breadsticks, a hot batch was coming straight out of the oven, mouthwatering garlic butter dripping off of them! With four garlic twists in hand, Charle headed past Kelly's Creamery and down a back alley. A breeze was gently blowing, which kept the sunny day from becoming too hot, and some wind chimes from one of the downtown apartments echoed between the buildings as he walked past.

The day was perfect for skipping stones at Lake Thompson's boat launch. So instead of going straight home, Charlie headed for the water. He always found the best flat rocks there. He made his way to the boat ramp and passed by Old Man Humphrey's house. It was a large house built in the late 1800s and had a lot of bends, turns, and odd shaped windows. Every time Charlie and his friends passed the house, they'd hear strange noises or see strange shadows in the windows. No one remembers seeing Old Man Humphrey in years. The adults in the area think the kids are being ridiculous, but everyone under the age of fourteen agrees something strange goes on in that house.

One time when Charlie and Ben, his best friend in the entire world, were walking home from school, they had just stepped past Old Man Humphrey's house when a cat jumped out of a tree onto Ben's backpack right as the front door of the house slammed shut! There was a moment of chaos as the boys escaped the cat attack. Charlie and Ben heard crying but didn't stick around to find out who or why. They ran almost the instant the cat lunged at Ben. Luckily they escaped with no injuries. It was just another confirmation that something strange went on at Old Man Humphrey's.

Charlie reached the boat launch at about a quarter past three. Since it was such a gorgeous day, plenty of people were out on the lake. Cars filled the parking lot, all of which had boat trailers. Off to the far left, one man gracefully paddled his yellow kayak across the water, which looked as smooth as glass. Directly in front, one man sped by on a jet ski, destroying the stillness and forcing waves to rock the man in the yellow boat. Fishing boats, speed boats, and pontoon boats scattered as far as Charlie could see. The lake was perfect for playing. It was large enough to accommodate everyone.

Charlie headed right for his favorite spot by the dock. On one side was a concrete ramp for the boats, and on the other side, the lake floor was covered in stones. This was the spot Charlie found the best rocks! He was getting pretty good at skimming them fifty feet across the water. When he first started, he could only skip once or twice, if at all. Now, Charlie could skip a stone six times before it sank into the lake.

As the hum of the jet ski filled the air, Charlie gathered together four smooth flat stones and placed them in his front pant's pocket. The best spot he found for throwing the rocks was by the picnic tables where swans usually gathered. Today, Charlie counted 23 swans! They were always so beautiful. He hated to disturb them.

Taking a stone from his pocket, Charlie placed it between his first three fingers, bent down, and threw it. One, two, three, four, five, six, thunk. Six skips! Just as he expected. He took the next stone, got it ready, and threw it. One, two, three, four, five, and the jet ski passed right in front of the stone, blocking his view! *Man!* Charlie thought, *That could have been seven skips!* Feeling a little frustrated, he took another stone from his pocket and prepared to throw it. This time he waited for the jet ski to go to the other side of the lake. He gave it a good toss, and the stone skipped one, two, three, four, but before he could count anymore, something twisted around his ankles, knocking him flat on his butt. It was the woman with the miniature poodle from Guy's Bakery! The dog got excited and ran toward the swans tangling its leash around Charlie's feet. By the time he looked to see his stone, there weren't even ripples in the water to tell where it had sunk. "Geeze, two times in a row," Charlie said out loud. The woman, thinking he was talking to her, apologized and helped him up.

Charlie checked his watch and saw that it was almost four o'clock. He decided to head home so his mom wouldn't worry. But before he left, he took one last stone and tossed it behind his back as he walked away. Charlie listened for the stone to hit the water, but it never did! He stopped dead in his tracks and spun around looking for where the rock should have landed in the water. He saw nothing, and there was no rock to be found by his feet, just sand and grass! *Weird!* Charlie thought as he scratched his head. Only living a few houses up from the boat launch, he ran home, excited to see his mom.

"Mom, I'm home!" Charlie shouted as he swung open the front door. "School was great! I can't wait until tomorrow. Ben and I are going to get some of the other guys to play basket . . ." Charlie stopped mid-word as he took notice of his surroundings. All the furniture had been covered with white sheets, and there were five suitcases piled in the foyer. Two were Charlie's.

"Oh! Hi, honey, you're home," Cathy Higgins said when she walked down the stairs. "I have a great surprise for you. We are going to spend the entire summer with Uncle Ralph and Auntie Phranzie at the seaside in England! Isn't that great? We leave in the morning."

Charlie stood staring at his mother in disbelief. "What?" he asked in shock.

"Well, aren't you going to thank me for a great summer vacation?" Cathy shamelessly asked.

"Thank you? You've ruined my summer! I thought . . . I'm supposed to . . . How could you and Dad do this to me? Can't you and Dad go by yourselves? I could stay with Ben if I ask his mom."

"No," Cathy said feeling hurt, "And your father isn't coming. He leaves tomorrow for a three-month business trip to China. It'll just be the two of us. I thought it would be a great way to spend time together. Especially with your big birthday coming up, I thought this could be a trip of a lifetime. Something momentous to mark your 13th birthday!"

Charlie stood looking at his mother thinking of every bad thing he wanted to say but didn't. *How could she do this to me?* He thought to himself. Without much control, Charlie yelled, "I hate you!" and threw down his backpack knocking over the carefully stacked suitcases. "No wonder Dad's always gone!" Charlie added as he ran up the stairs and slammed his bedroom door shut.

Cathy stood there in shock! She didn't like the fact that Ron was always gone on business trips. Ever since he took the new job, he'd been gone every other month for a few weeks to countries all over the world. Cathy felt like she barely knew her husband anymore and was trying the best she could to provide a fun summer for Charlie. Tears rolled down her cheeks as she picked up the knocked over suitcases.

Charlie threw himself on his bed with such force, the bed frame creaked. He was so mad his head hurt. He picked up his cell phone and called Ben to break the news. "What do you mean you are going to England in the morning? Can't you convince your Mom to have you stay with me?" Ben asked, obviously confused and disappointed. Unsatisfied with the phone conversation, Ben convinced Charlie to meet him at the McPherson Mansion so they could see each other one last time before he left. Charlie knew his mother wouldn't let him leave after a display like that, so he decided to sneak out. There was a perfect climbing tree right outside his window. He climbed down the tree as if he had done it many times, when in fact this was his first time ever sneaking out. Charlie's heart raced at the thought of getting caught, but with a thud that popped his cell phone out of his pocket, he successfully made it down the tree without his mom finding out!

Pacing impatiently under the giant maple tree behind the McPherson Mansion, Charlie waited. The mansion was a huge white structure that used to be home to a prominent family of the city many years ago, but now it only housed cobwebs and rodents. "He should have been here ten minutes ago!" Charlie muttered under his breath in frustration because he couldn't find his cell phone to call him. Ben was never late. Turns out, Ben got stuck watering his mother's enormous prize winning flower garden before he was allowed to leave. Since Charlie snuck out of his house and dropped his phone climbing out of the tree, Ben had no way of telling him that he'd be late. Charlie would just have to figure it out.

Five more minutes passed, and Charlie had had enough! He kicked a pine cone at the tree and stomped off. "What a crappy day! Even my best friend stands me up!" he shouted at nothing. Needing to calm down, Charlie decided to walk through the cemetery and sit by Lake Thompson away from any people. If it had not been for his current circumstances, he would have rather enjoyed the walk. The sky was bright blue with puffy white clouds scattered about. A subtle wind danced through the tree leaves. Squirrels hopped from one tree to the next, and the water sparkled reflections of the summer sun's rays. But all he could think about was how irritated he was with everyone's ignorance of his needs. His mom ruined his summer, and his best friend wasn't there for him when he needed him the most!

He took no notice of anything around him and just plopped down next to a tree letting out a big fed up "humph." Charlie didn't realize that a weathered fisherman was leaning against the other side of the same tree. The fisherman wore a vest and hat covered in lures and hooks. He had a short white beard and a gentle gleam in his eyes. His skin was dark and wrinkled from the many years he had sat by the water fishing. "Excuse me for being rude, but is something bothering you, son?" the fisherman asked. Charlie jumped! He was startled and took a minute to reply back.

"You wouldn't understand," Charlie shot back a bit embarrassed.

"You'll never know unless you tell me. That is, if you need to vent. I am unbiased. I don't know you or anything about you so, whatever you say, I'll give you honest feedback. If you think about it, I'm the best chance you got at feeling better."

All of a sudden Charlie felt his mouth open and blurted, "This stinks! I can't believe my mom thought leaving for the whole summer to stay with family I've never met would be fun. I mean, come on! What does she expect me to do all summer? Sip tea and sit up straight?" Charlie had never been so rude to a stranger before, but he needed to let out his thoughts. Catching himself, he extended his hand and said, "I'm sorry. I don't even know your name. I'm Charlie."

"The name's Tom. Nice to meet you, Charlie," he said extending his hand with an understanding grin."How about starting from the beginning?" So Charlie explained how the 13th birthday is monumental and how this summer was supposed to be the best summer he would ever have. He told Tom about his mother's plans to ruin it all by sending the two of them to England for the whole summer without asking his permission, and then to top it all off, his best friend doesn't show up so he could say good-bye. Tom sat for a minute taking it all in, then looked Charlie honestly in the eye and said, "Actually, I'm kind of jealous." Tom paused, "Think about it. You get to travel across the world to spend the summer meeting new people and learning about a different culture."

"What are you talking about?" Charlie asked feeling annoyed.

"I'm talking about the biggest adventure of your life! I guess it would be even better if Ben could come with you, but you'll have to get over it and then let yourself have fun," Tom explained.

"You feel pretty confident about that," Charlie said as he tried to feel out Tom. "I guess I'm just mad because this is the summer of my 13th birthday, and Mom and Dad always talked about that birthday being the most important. They told me, 'It's when you go from a boy to a young man.' I just wanted to have a say in how I wanted to spend my first summer as a young man. I guess it sounds pretty stupid," Charlie said looking down.

"No, not stupid, just selfish," Tom added.

"Hey!"

"Think about it. You're busy thinking about how your plans are ruined, but did you stop to think that your mom would rather spend the summer with her husband than with distant relatives? This has got to "stink," as you would say it, for her too."

Immediately, Charlie knew Tom was right, but he still felt he should have been allowed to make the final decision on the matter. Tom and Charlie sat talking for a few more minutes and then said good-bye. Charlie thanked Tom for his help and was glad he accidentally met him.

Running back home, hoping his mother hadn't gone upstairs to check on him, Charlie looked at his watch seeing that he had 15 minutes until dinner was ready. He had a much harder time climbing up the tree to his room than he did climbing down. *Had it really been that long since he climbed a tree?* Charlie thought. He made it into his room just as he heard his mother's footsteps coming up the stairs. Knock! Knock! Charlie jumped with fear thinking he'd been caught.

"Are you too angry for dinner?" Cathy asked through the door.

"No," Charlie mumbled.

"Good. Your father won't be home for an hour, but he said we can eat without him."

Charlie rolled his eyes, "Whatever, I'll be right down."

Things are just getting worse. Charlie thought. *You think my father would want to see me before we both depart across the world in different directions for the summer. Work must be SO much more important than spending time with his son. This is unfair!*

That night, Charlie and Cathy ate in silence. Cathy tried to think of all the possible reasons her husband must have had to spend the last night at the office instead of with his family. When it came down to the truth, Ron liked his job more than his family. Whether he would admit to it or not, Ron's actions proved true. As Charlie cleared his plate to leave the kitchen, Cathy spoke up saying, "Oh! I found your cell phone outside when I was watering the flower bushes. You must have dropped it playing there yesterday. I guess you won't be needing it for a while, anyway." Charlie froze in place staring blankly at her, cheeks burning from the fear of being caught. When she didn't say anything else about it, he headed to his room and went to bed without saying a word to his mother.

II

The Clock Maker

It was a long and torturous seven-hour flight from Detroit to Heathrow Airport. It wasn't the silent treatment he was giving his mother, the stuffy air, or even the large snoring lady who blocked the window view, that made the flight miserable. It was the bratty, 4-year-old, pig-tailed girl, that screamed and kicked his seat for the last three hours of the flight. Every time Charlie thought she was finished, she'd give a great big kick sending his head flying forward. Talk about unbearable!

Finally, after leaving the airport and the busy city traffic with roundabout after roundabout, Charlie found himself strangely enjoying the scenic views of the English countryside. By now, Charlie was mostly over being angry at his mother, even though he had not apologized yet. He felt comfortable enough in her presence to enjoy the day. With his head resting against the window, he marveled at the passenger trains that streamed alongside the road.

The speed and precision of the trains made Charlie envious of the riders.

Feeling jet-lagged, they finally arrived at the seaside town by late afternoon. The sun was still high in the sky, and the busyness of the earlier day had worn off. People were aimlessly strolling along the beach and leisurely flowing in and out of the local shops. All the pubs along the beach were full with hungry customers enjoying the cool breeze as they had tea on this unusually hot day. It was nearly 90 degrees, but the sea breeze made it pleasant. Cathy looked over at Charlie staring out the window and caught him smiling, but as soon as he saw his mother watching, he pulled his head away from the window and pretended not to smile. Charlie was not ready to admit that going to England might have been a good idea.

Passing through town, they reached the edge of the nature preserve and took a right. Charlie had forgotten Uncle Ralph and Auntie Phranzie lived next to a conservancy, and he itched for the chance to sneak away to explore! Pulling up in their driveway, Charlie noticed two things. First, the driveway was extremely steep. No one would be able to get up a driveway like that during a winter in Howell. Second, there were clocks strewn all around the front garden. At first Charlie only saw a few, but the more he looked, the more he saw! Pictures of clocks were stamped into the concrete, flower beds were arranged to look like clocks (all telling different times), and even the light post had a miniature working clock fabricated on it. At the front door, the knob, knocker, and door bell were all dressed with little clocks.

Auntie Phranzie was already at the door and pounced on them with big hugs and wet kisses. Boy! She was an interesting sight! Her curly red hair bounced with each movement and gesture. She wore librarian glasses, a floral dress with a lace collar, and plain black heels. Her lipstick was bright red, and she smelled like an old lady's perfume. *Great! Now I have lipstick on my cheek,* Charlie thought to himself as Auntie Phranzie planted a big wet kiss on his face. They were barely in the door when Charlie and Cathy were hurried to the kitchen for a pot of tea and cakes. Charlie rarely drank tea, but enticed by his aunt's English accent, Charlie had a cup of tea along with about five marzipan cakes of all different colors.

Right away, Auntie Phranzie chatted relentlessly about all the quilts she had made, was making, and was planning to make with the Women of Society Quilting Guild or the WSQG, as she liked to put it. When Charlie asked what a guild was, Auntie Phranzie straightened her posture, placed both her hands on her lap, and proudly explained, "We ladies of the Quilting Guild are a local group who meet daily to create masterpieces of fabric and thread. Highest honor among the sewing world, you know!" she said with a wink.

At that, Auntie Phranzie seized the moment to show off samples of her quilting to Cathy and Charlie. She gracefully stood up, walked across the kitchen, opened a low cupboard, and pulled out a rather large plastic bin. She dragged it across the floor, wiggling her rear end up in the air revealing that she was only wearing knee-high stockings. She snapped off the top of the bin to expose hundreds of swatches of fabric and a plethora of pattern books. Charlie took this distraction as an opportunity to slip away as quickly as possible!

Making his way to the family room, Charlie discovered the walls in the room were covered with many black and white portraits framed in carved wood. One frame had woodland animals, another was decorated with lilies and butterflies, and one, of course, had clocks. The frames were beautiful enough to hang alone. The portraits themselves consisted mostly of family memories. The frame with lilies and butterflies held a picture of Auntie Phranzie on her wedding day, and the one with clocks showcased what looked to be a young Uncle Ralph, not much older than ten, standing in the nature preserve. Charlie found this picture amusing. The scrawny and extremely freckled boy with a clumsy stance resembled himself. He stood examining the picture for several minutes and noticed a peculiar leather bound book with a strange clock on it tightly grasped under Uncle Ralph's left arm. Charlie leaned in to further examine the book when suddenly a hand grabbed his shoulder and spun him around! Charlie let out a scream! "A little jumpy, my boy," Uncle Ralph said, "was just wondering if Auntie Phranzie showed you your room?"

"Uhh . . . No, not yet," Charlie stuttered.

"Well then, lad, follow me." Charlie obeyed immediately, grabbing his suitcases and clumsily following Uncle Ralph down the main hall just stopping at the first bend. A door was cracked open to the left and then the hall continued down to the right ending at the bathroom. "Here we are, Charlie," Uncle Ralph puffed out. Not thinking much about it, Charlie took his things and headed into the room on his left only to find his face suddenly squished into a once partially opened door. "Mustn't go in there. That room is off-limits . . . even to Auntie Phranzie," Uncle Ralph said with a mischievous chuckle.

Puzzled and somewhat confused, Charlie looked around and asked, "Do you want me to sleep in the bathroom?" Without a verbal answer, Uncle Ralph looked up to the ceiling and smirked. There was an attic door with a white draw string.

"There you are, lad. You should have everything you need now." After patting Charlie on the shoulder and nearly knocking the suitcases out of his hands, Uncle Ralph turned around and disappeared into the forbidden room. The door was only open for a second, but Charlie was able to catch a glimpse of the far wall. It was covered in clock parts!

What's with the clock fixation? Charlie said to himself. Not putting any more thought into it, he looked up, grabbed a hold of the cord hanging from the ceiling, and pulled down the ladder. "Sweet!" Charlie exclaimed and climbed up.

III

The Attic Room

Surprisingly, the attic room was not dusty. Yes, it was dark and smelled a bit like mothballs but no dust. Auntie Phranzie was an avid cleaner as well as an avid quilter. When Charlie came up into the room, he noticed many old trunks and chests neatly stacked against the wall in front of him. There was just enough room to pull himself and his suitcases up. The floor was hard wood and made a clunk when the suitcases hit. The ceiling was also wood and had rafters that Charlie could touch if he stood on his toes. His bed was on the opposite side of the room and showcased an aged quilt.

Like any curious boy, Charlie began to investigate his surroundings. There were shelves with old books and gadgets from the early 1900s, a stack of old hats on a dresser, and two lace dresses on headless manikins. Next to his bed was a tall Victorian floor lamp that gave off a yellowish light, and on the other side of the bed was a nightstand with a flashlight and candle. Only one window existed in the attic, and it was on the wall by the night stand.

From the window, Charlie could see almost the entire nature preserve. It went on for miles in almost all directions. There were spots of forest both thick and thin, areas of clearing with tall grass, and many ponds, all different shades of blue and green. Wanting a better view, Charlie pulled the nightstand under the window and began to climb up on it. As he pulled his second foot up, he placed it on the flashlight and slipped sideways. Out of reflex, Charlie threw his arms in front of him and grabbed onto the windowsill hoping to catch his fall. What he didn't expect was for the windowsill to open. Charlie lost his grip and fell backward landing on the bed with a loud THUD!

From the level of the bed, Charlie could see that the windowsill opened to reveal a small cubby with something inside it. Getting off the bed, he carefully moved the nightstand back hoping nobody downstairs heard the commotion and took the mysterious object out of the windowsill. It was hard, covered in dust, and about the size of a large chocolate candy box. Unable to decipher what it was just by looking at it, Charlie took a deep breath and blew the dust making it fly everywhere. He could see that it was a leather book with a crest attached to the front cover. He took his sleeve and wiped the remaining dust off the crest, but it wasn't a crest at all! It was a strange looking clock!

The clock was approximately six inches in diameter and trimmed in gold. The numbers were Roman Numerals with twelve, three, six, and nine closer to the center of the clock than the other numbers. It was for the most part very simple looking but had an intrinsic mechanical design. The very center of the clock was glass, and underneath it looked to be gears and other pieces. Charlie put his ear to the clock and heard nothing. *It must be broken,* he thought.

Still staring at the book, he remembered he had seen this very book before. "The picture!" he gasped out loud. Charlie dropped the book on the bed. He scurried down the ladder, careful not to miss a step, as he ran into the family room. When he walked up to the wall, careful not to draw any attention, he discovered the picture was gone! It was replaced with another family portrait which was slightly smaller. The outline of the previous picture could still be seen in the faded wallpaper.

Right as Charlie made the discovery of the missing picture, Uncle Ralph walked in the room and asked, "Looking for something?"

Taken off guard, Charlie responded with, "Uh . . . No. I was just walking around." Not wanting to hear if Uncle Ralph had anything else to say, Charlie slipped past him and went back up to the attic room to look at the book. This time Charlie pulled up the ladder and cord to lock himself in. The book was sitting exactly where he left it. Unlike the picture downstairs, the book did not grow legs and walk off.

Charlie was beginning to feel very suspicious about Uncle Ralph and was certain he had something to do with the disappearing picture. Uncle Ralph had always been known as the odd uncle. He was a gray-haired man with a white mustache cushioning his upper lip. He wore sweaters and sweater vests that were probably knitted by Auntie Phranzie. Charlie recalled his mother saying things like, "Well you know Uncle Ralph," or, "That sounds like something Uncle Ralph would do."

Sitting on the bed with the book on his lap, Charlie struggled to open the strap that held the book closed. He tried pulling the strap, wiggling the strap, and ripping the strap. Nothing worked. Looking closely, Charlie discovered the strap fed into the clock. Puzzled, Charlie took the face of the clock and shook it to see if it would move. Nothing. *Maybe if I lift it,* he thought as he took the clock face and opened it like a book. Under the face was a latch that held down the leather piece. Charlie unhooked the latch and released the strap with a snap! The force of it opening blew more dust into Charlie's face causing him to cough and wipe his eyes.

By this point, Charlie's heart was beating quickly as if he had been waiting his whole life to see what was in this book. He opened the cover and read the hand written entry on the first page:

> *August 4, 1948*
> *If you are reading this entry, then I presume you have stumbled upon this book, and therefore should be warned that this is only for the serious. This is not a fool's toy or child's storybook. The information that lies between these pages will change your life. Only proceed if you understand the full consequences of your decision.*
>
> *I was walking in the nature preserve when I came across something strange. My hike had begun just like every other day. I said good-bye to mother and took the path from the house to the Duck Pond, but after arriving at the Duck Pond, something peculiar happened. Like always I searched for skipping stones and found about ten good ones. I began skipping the stones, and by the fourth stone I was skipping clear across the pond with little effort. At first, I thought all*

my practice had paid off and that I was finally ready to challenge the older school boys at a skipping contest. When I threw the fifth stone, it made it to the center of the pond and then vanished into thin air! Thinking I must have blinked and missed seeing the stone sink into the water, I took another stone and skipped it again, but that time it only made it a quarter of the way across the pond before vanishing in thin air! At this point, I still thought I must have blinked or got the glare of the sun in my eyes, because who has ever heard of vanishing stones? So I took another stone, and instead of skipping it, I threw it as far as I could across the pond. But before it went more than three feet in the air, it vanished! I stood for about five minutes trying to figure out what was happening to the stones. I tried to come up with a logical explanation such as, I needed glasses, or that I needed more sleep because I was beginning to hallucinate. The only idea I could come up with that made the most logical sense was it was unexplainable! I decided to throw the last three stones all at once as sort of an experiment. Two of the stones dropped in the water with a plop-plop, but the stone in the middle never made it over the water! So now I was curious. The missing stones had to be going somewhere, but where? I tried to calculate in my head the location and movement of the vanishing points. With every stone I threw, it vanished closer and closer to me as if something was moving towards me. Wanting to be brave, but mostly scared, I closed my eyes and stuck my hand out in front of me. I didn't feel anything

different, but when I opened my eyes I could only see my arm down to my elbow! The bottom half of my arm had disappeared as if I stuck it inside an invisible window. As far as I could tell, I could still wiggle my fingers, but I couldn't see my hand! Then my hand felt something. It was cool, smooth, and thick. I grabbed the object and pulled my hand out quickly hoping to snatch the object from inside this "invisible window." It was this book with a strange clock on it! Right away I was frightened that I had done something horribly wrong and was going to get in trouble. I tried to put it back, but when I reached my hand out, it didn't disappear. The "invisible window" was gone! I sat at the Duck Pond for a good hour contemplating what to do with the book. Should I hide it, should I destroy it, should I tell someone, or should I . . . open it? I carefully thought about it, and I came up with many reasons not to do it. Yet, it seemed like the book came to me and that sort of gave me a right to look inside. So when I decided to open the book, the clock on the cover, as if reading my thoughts, began ticking a strange tick-tock, tick-tick, tock-tock rhythm. The rest you can read for yourself. Proceed carefully. You will NEVER be the same!
Ralph Higgins

Charlie was blown away! *A magical book? Could this really be a supernatural book?* He asked himself. Then Charlie realized that when he opened the book, the clock did not tick. "Perhaps it is just old and full of dust," he said, and turned the first page.

IV

Wenzel Bennington

The smell of the pages was sweet. They were a tan color, possibly made from grass. Charlie had expected the pages to smell musty like the secret cubby he found it in. *All part of being a magical book,* Charlie thought.

The first chapter of the book was titled "Wenzel Bennington." *Nothing too life-changing about that title, Charlie* thought. He took the bed pillows and propped them up behind his back. He glanced over at the attic door in the floor to make sure there was no way someone could accidentally sneak up on him. Assured no one could get up into the attic without him knowing, Charlie began to read:

It was a perfectly sunny day as Wenzel Bennington sat against the giant oak tree that stood in the center of the village. Everyone knew the tree and called it "The Great Oak." It stood there and had been that big for as long as anyone's grandparents' grandparents could remember. Never did the tree look limp, bare, or sick. The Great Oak was always lush with giant green leaves covering its branches, and the bark showed not a scratch, peel, or wound of any kind. Its shade gave refreshment from the sun on days where it was slightly too warm. Where Wenzel lived, there was never an awful day . . . until now.

Wenzel leaned up against the tree with his head tilted up to the sky. He closed his eyes and let the brightness of the day dance shadows through his eyelids. Wenzel smiled to himself with bliss. He loved his life. Even though he did not remember his mother and father, his Aunt Trudy and Uncle Lucas were the best parents he had known. His childhood was happy, and now that he was a young man of 19, he was ready to start a life of his own. While shadows danced before his eyes, Wenzel began to daydream of faraway lands and mighty adventures. Often, Aunt Trudy would tell him that his imagination was too wild and bound to get him in trouble, but Wenzel disagreed. He loved to pretend he was part of something bigger than himself and his quaint life living on The Hill. Still, he was perfectly content and happy. Suddenly a shadow considerably darker than the others appeared. It stuck out against everything around it. So much so that Wenzel immediately opened his eyes and did a double-take. It was the ugliest bird he had ever seen! The wings were mangled, and the body was practically bald except for a few feathers fighting to stay on. The beak was misshapen, and the head had several small bulges making it look like a lump of clay. Either Wenzel was seeing things, or this bird was lost. No animals in the Village had ever looked like that. Not even the ones that were close to death! That bird was not from around here. Wenzel was confused as he stared at the bird perched on the branch of The Great Oak. Then suddenly, as if the bird could hear Wenzel's thoughts, it turned its ugly head and looked him directly in his eyes! Chills went down Wenzel's spine. The bird squinted at Wenzel as if saying, "I see you," and then flew away. If that was not strange enough, the branch that it was sitting on was now completely dead! The golden brown drained from the bark of the branch right before Wenzel's eyes, causing the leaves to dry up and fall to the ground! Panicked, Wenzel jumped up and ran home to tell his aunt and uncle.

Crash! Thunder struck outside the attic window. Charlie had been so occupied by the book that he failed to notice the storm approaching from the nature preserve. Then he realized someone had been calling his name. "Charlie! Charlie! Are you alright up there?" It was his mom. Charlie closed the book, hid it under his pillow, and ran to unlock the attic door. He opened it and saw that his mother and Auntie Phranzie were standing in the hallway staring up at him.

"Yeah, I'm fine, Mom. Why?"

"A strange storm has blown in from the English Channel. It looks like it's going to be nasty, and I wanted to make sure you weren't frightened."

"I'm almost thirteen, Mom. I'm okay. It looks like a typical thunderstorm to me."

"That's just it," chimed in Auntie Phranzie, "We don't get storms like this, at least not since I was a child. Best be cautious is all."

"Okay. Is that it?"

"Yes, Charlie. What are you doing up there anyway? You disappeared as soon as Auntie Phranzie began to talk about quilts, and Uncle Ralph said you'd been up in the attic for most of the evening."

"Oh, I'm just relaxing. I'm reading a good book I, ah, um, found."

"Good for you, honey! I knew this trip was going to be beneficial to you! Well, if you need anything, let us know. Otherwise, I'll see you in the morning."

"Goodnight," Charlie blurted, then closed and locked the attic door again.

By now the storm was in full force. The rain drops pelted the attic window, the wind howled like a ravenous dark creature, and the lightning lit up the sky as the thunder echoed its actions. Charlie felt a little scared when he stood looking out the window. With each flash of lightning Charlie could see his reflection, and then the room would go dark again. Then Charlie heard a voice in his mind. At first he thought it was just a thought, but then he heard it again! "Grab the book," the voice said. Not quite understanding what was going on, Charlie grabbed the book from under his pillow and stood back by the window once again watching the lightning light up the sky. Suddenly the lightning and rain calmed.

It was only for a few moments and then BOOM! The lightning and thunder struck simultaneously. In fact, the lightning was so strong, it reached through the attic window, and struck the clock on the face of the book throwing Charlie across the room! He hit his head on an old trunk box knocking him out, and the book slid across the room. At that instant, the storm went completely silent. "Charlie! Charlie! What is going on up there?! Charlie!" his mother yelled as she hit the attic door with a broom handle.

The banging of the broom woke Charlie from his stupor. Not knowing what just happened, Charlie stumbled toward the book, grabbed it, and hid it behind his back as he opened the attic door. "What, Mom?" he said irritated he hit his head and slightly annoyed she was bothering him again.

"I heard a big crash. Are you okay?" Cathy asked in a panic.

"Um . . . I just tripped. I'm really jet lagged. I'm, I'm okay."

"Are sure? Because if you're hungry, or it's too much sleeping up there by yourself, I can make a bed on the . . ."

"Mom, I'm fine, just fine," Charlie interrupted, "I don't need anything. I want to sleep up here anyway. It's pretty cool." At that, Charlie's mom nodded and blew him a kiss.

"Good night, Mom," he said and shut the attic door. Charlie took the book to the bed and paused as he looked down and saw the small gears moving and heard *tick-tock, tick-tick, tock-tock, tick-tock, tick-tick, tock-tock.*

V

The Clock Room

The next morning Charlie woke up feeling surprisingly refreshed. With traveling all day the day before, and the episode with the storm, he had expected to feel exhausted. He checked to make sure the book was still under his pillow (it was) and then hurriedly got dressed. Just before he opened the attic door, he took the book from behind his pillow and tucked it into his backpack. He then headed down the attic ladder ready to go explore the nature preserve. *Today is a perfect day for an adventure,* he thought. *Not only do I get to explore the conservancy, but I can read this book without any distractions!*

It was about nine in the morning and Charlie could hear Uncle Ralph stirring around in the forbidden room. This time the door was completely shut, and Charlie could only guess what Uncle Ralph was up to. With his stomach growling, Charlie entered the kitchen ready to devour the entire refrigerator, but he stopped in his tracks as he looked at who was sitting at the kitchen table! Auntie Phranzie was there, of course, and dressed in her skirt and blouse with a hundred WSQG patches. Each one depicted a symbol marking one of Auntie Phranzie's many quilting accomplishments. Charlie had to admit, though it was embarrassing, she made some pretty outstanding quilts. But that could not have prepared him for who sat across the table from her. With his mouth gaping open wide, he stared at his mother, Cathy Higgins, who was dressed identically to Auntie Phranzie! The only difference was that Cathy didn't have nearly as many patches.

"Good morning, Charlie," a very cheery Cathy said.

"Hi," Charlie shockingly replied not quite sure what to make of his mother's new look.

"There are cakes on the counter if you want to help yourself, or you can make some cereal," Auntie Phranzie jumped in.

Charlie was too busy staring at his mother to reply but grabbed a cake and slowly backed out of the kitchen. *That was weird!* Charlie thought to himself. *A lot of strange things are happening here.* With that, he plopped himself down on the family room couch and devoured the last of his cake. Licking the strawberry frosting off his fingers, Charlie looked up catching a glimpse of Uncle Ralph's forbidden room. The door was wide open! Not sure if it was a trick, Charlie quietly and slyly crept his way to the door along the wall holding his backpack across his chest. When he reached the door, he strained his head to peek inside without being seen. Right away he noticed that Uncle Ralph was gone! After looking around to see if he could spot him, Charlie slipped into the room. As soon as he got both feet into the room, the door slammed behind him and locked. Charlie jumped with fear nearly knocking over a table of small tools, gears, and cogs.

Sure that someone heard that, Charlie ran to the door and tried to open it. He knew he was in trouble now! Someone must have heard him! Then as if nothing worse could happen, he heard Uncle Ralph's footsteps coming to the door. In a frantic panic, Charlie dove under a table against the wall. He had to hide quickly! The force of diving under the table bumped open a small hidden door. Charlie had no time to think because Uncle Ralph began to turn the door handle! Charlie jumped into the hidden door and shut it behind him, leaving him in complete darkness! Breathing heavily, the only sound that he could hear now was his heart rapidly beating in his chest. Absolutely terrified he'd get caught, Charlie frantically began feeling around for another way out. Getting caught was not an option! *There must be a way outside from here.* Charlie tried to convince himself. A little frightened that he might stick his hands in a nasty spider web, he was relieved to find that the little room he was in continued on behind him. With his backpack securely on, he began to crawl on the dirt floor toward that back of the narrow dark room.

Every few inches forward, Charlie expected to hit a wall and hopefully another hidden door. But the further he went, the room continued on. He tried to stand but was met only with a low dirt ceiling. Crawling was his best and fastest option. With no other choice, Charlie trudged on knowing this pitch dark tunnel must lead somewhere!

VI

The Island of the Wyse

Mr. Littleston hid his lantern under his cloak as he snuck past the village square. He made sure that no one was following him as he approached the shore of Lake Wiliby. The night was calm, and the crescent moon shown brightly in the night sky. Quickly and quietly, Mr. Littleston uncovered his hidden row boat, pushed it to the water, and hopped in. He placed his lantern on the floor of the boat until he was far enough offshore not to be seen. He followed the shoreline until it bent, then he headed straight for the island. To Mr. Littleston's knowledge, he was the only one aware of the island. It was not visible from shore. In fact, he would have never found it if not for a strange current taking him there several weeks ago during a fishing trip.

On the island, Mr. Littleston secured his boat and took the path that led down a hall of massive pine trees. The pine trees lined the trail on both sides. Its prickly branches created a canopy that nearly blocked all the moon's light. With lantern in hand, Mr.

Littleston pushed through the ivy-covered gate at the end of the hall and headed up the stone stairs. At the top was a beautiful estate, and at the door, there she was waiting for him.

Back at the boat, Wenzel uncovered himself from the burlap tarp. He had been peeking out of the boat waiting for Mr. Littleston to disappear from sight. Wenzel crept out carefully as not to make any excessive noise. The air was cool and the sound of the waves crashing on the shore made him feel nervous. He wanted to see what Mr. Littleston had been up to. For weeks now, Mr. Littleston had been acting strangely. Normally, he kept to himself, but lately he was more secretive than usual. When Wenzel made his daily visits to see him, he acted nervously and looked as if he hadn't been sleeping. Now that Wenzel had seen that strange deformed bird, he decided to follow Mr. Littleston to see what was really going on!

With a dagger in his belt, Wenzel made his way toward the hall of pines. Not having a lantern and with the trees blocking the moonlight, Wenzel tripped over several fallen branches scraping up his arms and legs. By the time he made it to the stone steps, the coverage from the branches thinned enough for a bit of moonlight to guide his way. He pushed opened the ivy-covered gate and headed up the stairs. The beautiful estate caught Wenzel by surprise. He had never imagined such a grand place in his whole life. *How could no one else know of this till now?* he thought suspiciously.

Wenzel cautiously approached the building and placed himself flat against an exterior wall making sure no one could see him. Suddenly a light appeared in the window right next to Wenzel's head! He jumped down and hid behind a bush. From inside he could hear two voices. One was Mr. Littleston's and one was a woman he had never heard before. The conversation sounded tense!

"What happened, Mr. Littleston?" The woman sternly asked.

"Na, na nothing, my Lady," Mr. Littleston stuttered in reply.

"This has Malek's name all over it, and I think you are keeping secrets," she replied.

"I would not keep anything from you, my Lady, you have my, um, word!" he exclaimed.

There was a long silence. It made Wenzel uncomfortable. *Who is Malek? Who is this woman? Is she the reason the Great Oak is dying?* Wenzel could not steady his mind much longer. He had to see who Mr. Littleston was talking to!

Very slowly, Wenzel stood up and carefully peered through the side of the window. He saw Mr. Littleston's back as he stood facing a corner of the room that was just out of sight. Wenzel was going to have to reposition himself to get a better view. While holding his breath, he ducked down and ran to the other side of the window and laid flat against the wall of the estate again. This spot would give him full view of the corner the woman was in.

Suddenly, he heard the woman scream! Wenzel looked through the window to see Mr. Littleston with his hand around her neck! Without hesitation, Wenzel forced opened the window and pulled out his dagger. The sound of the window caused Mr. Littleston to turn his head giving the woman enough time to push him off her. Wenzel then jumped through the window and tackled Mr. Littleston, pinning him to the floor with the dagger pressed firmly on his neck. Once again, the room fell silent except for everyone's heavy breathing. Wenzel was not sure why he reacted the way he did. He did not know this woman. She could be the reason the Hill is falling apart, and why Mr. Littleston had been acting so strangely.

Mr. Littleston began to cry. It was not a sad and regretful cry, but a painful cry. Wenzel at first thought he had injured the man, but something told him there was a darkness at work!

"Move, Wenzel!" the woman shouted. Without hesitation, Wenzel obeyed, and just in time, too! As soon as Wenzel lifted his body off of Mr. Littleston, a bright light flashed making Mr. Littleston disappear! Wenzel fell to the floor and just stared at the spot his former friend had occupied.

Then, a kind hand touched his shoulder and assisted him to a chair. Waiting on the side table was a cup of hot tea. "Thank you," she said, "I knew he had let darkness in."

Wenzel sipped the tea listening, then stopped to ask demandingly, "How did you know my name?"

The woman smirked and said, "Because I'm the Wyse of this land, and it is my job to know the name of the one who will come by my window with a dagger in hand to save my life. You see, Wenzel, there are greater forces at work than just you and me."

Wenzel took a minute to digest her words and glanced around the room. He just wasn't sure what to think anymore. It was a very large white room filled floor to ceiling with books and scrolls. A grand table with one chair stood to his left, and a fireplace and comfortable chairs were arranged to his right. The table was covered in opened books and scrolls. Candelabras were scattered everywhere with partial candle sticks in them, all currently lit, wax dripping on the floor.

"From the looks of this room, you must read a lot," Wenzel commented sarcastically trying to break the awkward silence.

"That is a correct observation. A Wyse, such as myself, is a scholar who studies a land's history and prophecies. We keep our identities a secret to protect the land we observe. Our role is to be an assistance if history takes a drastic turn, and it has, Wenzel" she explained giving him a grave stare.

"Are there more of you?"

"Yes, all over this world. I am the only one here."

The Wyse and Wenzel sat talking for a couple more hours. Although Wenzel was extremely tired, the adrenaline rush of what had just happened, falsely kept him awake. By the time the second hour passed, Wenzel could feel a giant yawn sneaking up. "I should probably head home now. My aunt and uncle will worry if I am not in bed when they wake up," Wenzel said, starting to stand up.

"I do not think you understand what just happened here," she warned stepping in his way. "There is no going back. It has already begun! Spies have already been sent to look for you. Malek wants you dead. It is not safe for you to go back!" Wenzel stood with a shocked look on his face trying to figure out what to think.

"If I can't go back," he said, "What will happen to my aunt and uncle?"

"You must trust the Presence to take care of them. It was him who arranged that they would raise you in the first place. Have faith Wenzel. This is bigger than us," she said looking at a dumbfounded

Wenzel. Without a chance to reply, she gestured to the door and continued, "My servant will show you to your room. In the morning, you will begin your first training assignment. The instructions are in your room as well as everything you need. Take care Wenzel, the Hill needs you. You have been chosen by the Presence of this world to fight the darkness. Do not tread lightly or it will devour you." At that, the Wyse turned and left the room. Still digesting the Wyse's words, Wenzel stood for a minute flabbergasted before following the servant to his room.

VII

First Encounter

Wenzel sat against a tall birch tree contemplating his current predicament. He had barely gotten a grip on what just happened and had only just met the Wyse before she sent him away for a week-long solitude assignment. Bored, Wenzel took his sword and lazily drew pictures in the dirt. "What could I possibly learn out here?" he asked out loud rather annoyed. He had been sitting for hours and not even a bird had flown by. Suddenly, the bushes by the shore rustled loudly. Wenzel jumped to his feet and held his sword defensively waiting to attack whatever dark creature awaited him. Wenzel's adrenaline pumped as he imagined a large, and most likely meat-eating creature hiding in the bush! With his chest pounding, he slowly stepped forward never taking his eyes off the moving leaves. As soon as Wenzel got into reach of the bush, Charlie Higgins stood up! Immediately, Wenzel grabbed Charlie and pinned him down to the ground with his knee and sword landing Charlie hard on his backpack. "Identify yourself!" Wenzel demanded, his voice cracking with fear.

"Uh, um, Charlie!" he blurted.

"Tell me who sent you or I'll kill you!" shouted Wenzel.

"Uh, nobody. I . . .I . . .I just followed a tunnel here from my uncle's house. I didn't know this was private property . . ." Charlie said, looking around confused.

"That's enough," Wenzel cut him off. Not sure what to think and seeing that Charlie was unarmed, he helped him up saying, "Sorry, I have to be on guard. You understand."

"I'm not sure I do," Charlie uttered and brushed himself off.

Bewildered by Charlie's last remark, Wenzel prodded, "Where did you say you were from?"

"My Uncle Ralph's near the preserve. Are we close by?"

"You tell me. You are the one who crawled here," Wenzel stated pointing at Charlie's soiled hands and knees.

"Um, I guess I'll just go back," Charlie blurted out uncomfortably as he headed back to the bush. He moved the leaves aside trying to find where the tunnel was but could not see it. Thinking that he had the wrong bush, Charlie searched the one next to it, then another, then another, and another. Each time he became more frantic. "What is going on here?!" he exclaimed in a panicked voice.

Wenzel was now perplexed as well and examined the bushes curiously with Charlie. Having no other explanation, he said, "It is time to take you to the Wyse." At that statement, Charlie's heart sank.

He realized now he wasn't close to the preserve. In the pit of his stomach, Charlie knew he wasn't in England anymore . . .

■ ■ ■

The Wyse was dressed in a lace ivory gown showcasing a stiff collar. She sat perfectly upright in her tall back chair. Her hair was neatly pinned up and the cuffs of her sleeves came down to a point on the back of her hands. Her appearance was intimidating, to say the least. Charlie's heart pounded as Wenzel guided him down the corridor. With a stoic face, the Wyse sat locking her eyes on Charlie the whole time, watching his every move as he approached her.

"Congratulations, on completing your first training assignment," the Wyse said quickly switching her glance to Wenzel. "It has been said that when the Great Oak begins to die, one from another world will appear." The look on Charlie's face surprised the Wyse, and she said, "What is it young man?"

"I'm sorry. You must mean someone else. I didn't mean to come. I . . .I . . .I just um, crawled here from my uncle's secret . . .weird . . .clock room," Charlie said feeling stupid as he stumbled over his words.

"But you are not from the Hill or our world, and since no one has ever come before, it leaves me no other choice to believe but that you are the chosen one." The Wyse sat a moment contemplating how much more to reveal to Wenzel and Charlie and glancing at

Charlie's backpack, continued, "There will be others who will help you. Some who are friends and some who are foes. Sometimes, you will not be able to tell the difference. If you complete the task, you will save the Hill from complete destruction. Even as we speak, the Long Necks are leaving. That is not a good sign! Death is coming to the Hill!"

With that, the Wyse stood up from her seat and left the room with an abrupt and quickened pace. "Who are the Long Necks?" Charlie asked Wenzel who was now the only thing close to a friend.

"They are a quiet and peaceful animal. They only dwell in places that are calm and happy, and they can sense danger before anyone else. If the Long Necks leave a land, it is not good!" Wenzel explained as he pointed to a carving of them on the wall. The creatures looked a foot taller than a human with a bird-like face, long neck, furry arms and bodies, and two long human-like legs. With a peaceful appearance, Charlie could see that their only defense was to leave before harm approached. Whatever Charlie just crawled himself into, it was not good!

Then from out the window, Charlie and Wenzel heard a horn blowing towards the sea. Both of them ran to see what was going on and saw the Wyse blowing an ivory colored shofar covered in precious stones. The sound became so loud that it vibrated their bodies causing them to cover their ears and lose their step.

VIII

The Council of the Wyse

The following morning, the sun was warm and bright as it crept into Charlie's room. Half-thinking he was back at Uncle Ralph's and Aunt Phranzie's, he opened one eye to see if it had all been a dream. It had not. Drowsily, Charlie picked up his head off the pillow and sat in bed with his legs hanging to the side waiting for enough energy to stand up. This whole experience had drained him. Checking to see if his backpack was still under the pillow, he pulled it out and hugged it as he sat with his eyes closed again still hoping it was all just a nightmare. Rubbing his eyes, he caught sight of something out the window. Far off in the horizon, Charlie could see what looked like specks all over the ocean. Putting some slippers on and carrying his backpack, he curiously walked to the window, unlocked the hinge, and pushed it open. A cool sea breeze whirled passed him filling the room with fresh, salty air. He stuck his head out and studied the specks. They were ships! Hundreds of ships were coming this way! Charlie quickly dressed in the clothes laid out for him and ran to find Wenzel and the Wyse.

■ ■ ■

By supper time, all the ships had reached the island and hundreds of rowboats were making their way to the shore. Wenzel and Charlie joined the Wyse in the grand corridor for the arrival ceremony of all the Wyse from the allied lands. Ornate wooden chairs and tables were set up with an aisle down the center. The Wyse of the Hill, Wenzel, and Charlie were seated on the platform at the front of the chairs. As soon as the procession of the Wyse began, the three of them stood up. The Wyse of the Hill stood dressed in a velvet purple dress. Her high collar and pointed sleeves gave her an air of royalty, her stern face and poise added to it. Charlie could not believe his eyes! Men and woman with all different skin tones and features began to fill the place as the Wyse of the Hill's servants played music. All of the Wyse wore robes representing their area of the world. Each one wore a unique headdress to match. Some even held staffs, maces, or swords. Wenzel had never seen anything like this before. Up until just recently, he didn't know they even existed, and now he was standing in front of all the Wyse of the world, receiving them as guests!

As soon as the last Wyse arrived, the tall heavy doors shut with a thud, and every Wyse stood by a seat facing the trio on the platform. "Welcome, my friends, my colleagues, my like-minded men and woman. I have prepared a feast for you in honor of your long journey to get here, and your much needed counsel. Before you, stand two prophesies that have come into existence. It is time that we discuss our next move. I pray that the food replenishes your body and spirit so that we can be sharp at our work. You may be seated," the Wyse concluded and then sat down. She looked at the servant to her right and gestured a nod. At that, the servant blew a quiet whistle that Charlie could barely hear and instantly fifty other ornately-dressed servants entered pushing carts of delicious smelling food around to the tables. Wenzel had never seen so much food before in his life! Within minutes, every person in the room had a plate of food and drink. The corridor smelled of roasted meats, potatoes, sautéed vegetables, warm bread, savory rolls, and sweet cakes. After everyone had eaten their fill, they were dismissed to their rooms for the night. The council would be held in the morning.

IX

Evil Enters In

All the Wyse were gathered, well-rested, and ready to discuss the emergency council the Wyse of the Hill had summoned. The topic of concern was how evil had entered the Hill. So many generations had lived there without any threat of war. So, why now? What had changed?

The Wyse of the Hill explained:

"Mr. Littleston was a companion of mine and would secretly visit me. No one else knew of my existence. He accidentally traveled here when his fishing boat caught a new current and drifted to my island. One day he asked me to tell him who the chosen one to protect the Hill was. I did not know how he even knew such a person existed. I knew at that point, something in the Hill had changed. Knowing the power such information would give to Mr. Littleston, I refused to give him the answer. His spirit was weak. My refusal made him burn with anger. So, I decided to follow him.

I traveled by night and disguised myself as a farmer and watched him for a couple of weeks.

On one of those days, Mr. Littleston was alone in his garden when the most peculiar bird landed on a tree branch hanging over his head. It was a beautiful bird. It sat perched elegantly on the branch with the sun gleaming on its feathers, making them glisten in hues of red, green, and gold. Mr. Littleston slowly approached the bird, partially because he didn't want it to fly away and partially because he was awe-struck.

But when Mr. Littleston came within a foot of the bird, it spoke, catching the man, and myself, off-guard. 'I'm glad I've found you, Mr. Littleston,' the bird said. Shocked the bird knew his name, Mr. Littleston stepped back. No one has ever heard of talking animals!

'This must be a dream,' Mr. Littleston reassured himself aloud.

'Then why can you feel this?' At once, the bird flew from its branch and pecked the man on the head. 'Now will you listen to me,' it cackled, 'before I leave this sorry place?' At that point, Mr. Littleston was too baffled to take notice of the small voice in his head warning him of danger. I could hear it, too. The man sat for hours each day listening to the beautiful bird talk. He neglected all his chores to spend time with the bird. At first the bird entertained him with clever tricks, and then the bird began to ask him a few questions, questions he had been longing to hear. 'Do you want to know the name of the chosen one?' It asked.

'Yes! But she . . .I mean, I can't seem to figure it out.' Mr. Littleston blurted nearly giving away my existence.

'I thought so,' it said and then flew away.

Mr. Littleston ran after the beautiful bird with rage. He surprised himself with his emotion. The rest of the day and all that night, the man could not get the bird out of his head! It was all he could think about. It consumed him.

Early the next morning, Mr. Littleston ran out to his garden hoping to find the bird waiting for him. I was there watching. It wasn't. He was mad, and stomped at the ground! He had no motivation to do anything until he saw that bird again. He didn't eat, get dressed, or start his chores. He didn't even feel like visiting me. He craved the bird.

Finally, after several days, the bird arrived. Mr. Littleston was ecstatic and ran up to the bird nearly grabbing it. 'Back off fool!' it shouted. 'I have something you want little man.' Mr. Littleston stopped in his tracks. His heart began to race because he knew the bird would tell him!

"Then tell me. Please!' he said impatiently.

'I will,' the bird said snobbishly, then flew away again. Mr. Littleston ran to the tree nearly running up it.

'No!' he blurted angrily. He could not believe that the bird left him again. Day after day the bird came to the man, and day after day the man lost interest in his responsibilities and me. What the man did not notice, was the gradual changing appearance of the bird. It no longer gleamed. In fact, it was very ugly and deformed. Mr. Littleston's desperate desire of being with the bird blinded him from the gradual change.

Finally, the day came that the man had been waiting for! The bird was confident it had Mr. Littleston in his complete control because its beautiful disguise was completely gone, and Mr. Littleston still addressed him as 'beautiful bird.'

'Today's the day I'll tell you,' it heckled, 'and what you do with it is up to you.' The bird also knew the man's weakness. Without delay, the bird demeaningly said, 'It is none but little Wenzel! Now you know . . . was it worth it because now your loyalty belongs to the one who sent me!' It wickedly laughed and flew away.

Instantly Mr. Littleston was filled with guilt! He knew what he had done! He had just given himself over to the enemy of The Hill, to Malek! The one I'd been warning him about. That day, Mr. Littleston betrayed not only me but the entire Hill.

Then, as I have told you before, he came here to kill me and disappeared. This is very grave, my councilmen."

The whole council began murmuring to each other at the news of Malek entering the Hill. It had never happened before! It was impossible! Wenzel sat with his mouth open in shock! That bird, the spy of Malek, saw him with his own eyes! Chills ran down his body. This was serious!

X

Darkness Engulfs

The biggest storm that ever hit the Hill was about to make landfall. All the town's people were gathered under the withering Great Oak and were in imminent danger of being blown away. Aunt Trudy and Uncle Lucas were frantically looking for Wenzel. "Wenzel! Where are you?" they shouted over the crowd. Fear had taken over the Village! Wenzel and Mr. Littleston had mysteriously disappeared and now this! The villagers gathered together to seek comfort and safety, unaware of the intensity of the storm approaching from Malek's dark magic. With all the people crowded under the tree, the storm struck! The wind fiercely howled blowing out all their lanterns and candles leaving them in total darkness! The rain that had threatened them all day angrily poured down from the sky. The townspeople held tightly to one another afraid they'd get swept away. It lasted for several terrifying minutes then abruptly stopped, leaving everyone in an eerie dark silence. All of a sudden, out of nowhere, there was a loud crash of thunder! It sent all the people screaming and running in a panic! Unearthly screeches erupted from the darkness. Some people ran toward their homes to light lanterns, but others were driven crazy by fear and ran further into the darkness and were never seen again. They were engulfed by the creatures of the night. Those who ran toward the lighted lanterns were spared. The creatures hate the light.

By morning, the devastation of the storm was sadly realized. Houses had collapsed, roads were flooded, animals were loosened from their cages and pens—but the most devastating destruction was what lay in the middle of the village. The mighty Great Oak, the symbol of the wholeness and peace in the Village, was completely uprooted and lying on its side! The very thing that stood for their happiness and tranquility was dead and violated before them. Waves of sobbing and wailing could be heard day and night. Family members were missing and injured. Food and clean water were scarce. They needed a plan, and they had to act fast. It was time to flee the Hill and into the unknown. It became clear, that life was no longer what it once had been for the townspeople of the Hill.

With heavy hearts, Aunt Trudy and Uncle Lucas searched through the rubble that had once been their home. Overwhelmed with emotions, they searched through the house for anything worth taking with them. They had raised Wenzel there, and every brush of the rubble was a crumbled memory. Not knowing what had happened to Wenzel, they assumed the worst and that he would never be found again. With tear-stained cheeks, they packed what was left of their belongings and gathered with the remaining townspeople. Life was over there, and now they were to search for a new home, a new life, without Wenzel.

Rows of sullen townspeople lined up where the Great Oak once stood. Not quite sure where to go, they stood waiting for someone to start walking somewhere, anywhere. Suddenly, a strong wind came and swirled its way past the crowd of people. The wind swooped down to the ground and blew away a few inches of top soil to reveal a dark clay path. Having no other good options, and feeling a strange peace, the weary townspeople followed the path until nightfall. Each morning, the wind appeared and revealed a new path, and every night the path ended near clean water and food.

XI

The Commissioning

By now, the council had been in deliberation for days. Wenzel and Charlie had been asked to leave due to the sensitive nature of the discussion. Charlie barely had any time to think about what was happening to him, how he had apparently left England behind, how the strange book from Uncle Ralph's attic played a part in this, or who all these strange new people were. His head ached from the multitude of thoughts swimming around in his mind!

Wenzel anxiously paced outside the closed corridor doors. His mind, too, was racing a mile a minute. Once in a while he would pause, look up at Charlie sitting on the lounge chair by the window, and then continue pacing with more vigor. From what Charlie could tell, things were not going to calm down for them. They had received a report of the storm that destroyed the Great Oak, and then today they heard that all the townspeople had fled the Hill! Something jumped in Charlie's spirit as he thought about what was happening. He felt an unknown urgency to help, like he was created for this. Charlie could not explain the things going on around him, but all he knew was he needed to protect whatever was left of the Hill!

At 8 o'clock in the evening on the third day, the doors of the corridor swung open, and Charlie and Wenzel were summoned to the platform. Quick on their feet, they both made their way to the front of the corridor. There, standing before them was an even sterner looking Wyse of the Hill. Worry and concern wrinkled her face. The stress of the past few days had obviously aged her. This was serious! With her eyes fixed on Wenzel and Charlie, she said, "It is our decision with the best interest of the Hill in mind that we will send you away for further training. Now that the townspeople have evacuated the Hill and Malek has yet to make a march towards the Hill, we have decided to send you with the Wyse of the Lonely Manor. There you will be trained in combat, discernment, survival, herbology, and how to recognize dark magic, though you yourselves will never use any. You will depart in the morning."

Wenzel and Charlie glanced at each other with confidence in their new task. From deep within, both felt responsible for accepting their fate and doing whatever possible to save the Hill. "Do you accept?" the Wyse loudly asked.

Unanimously they answered, "We do!" At that, the room filled with noise of shuffling chairs and feet. Soon Wenzel and Charlie were surrounded by all the Wyse. Each extended an arm, a sword, a staff, or a mace touching Wenzel and Charlie if possible. Those that could not reach them, touched the person closest to them. Instantly, everyone was connected.

"We charge you Wenzel and Charlie to take the task before you with bravery and courage, to always do what is right even when it does not make sense to do so. May you always adhere to your teachings, seek the Presence for guidance and help, and never stray from your gut instinct. May you be successful in your journey and save the Hill from being captured by Malek. For if he succeeds, we are all doomed to the same fate. Fear not what your eyes see, and may you find security in what your spirit tells you. We stand behind you, Wenzel and Charlie. Though we cannot go with you, we are fighting for you. May the power of unity strengthen you as you leave this place."

The Wyse lowered her hands and stepped off the platform. She placed her hands on the Wyse in front of her and everyone shouted, "So be it!" In an instant a warm glow flowed through the crowd and into Wenzel and Charlie. It was strong and powerful as it traveled through Wenzel and Charlie from head-to-toe. The strength of it overcame them, and they collapsed to the floor. At that, all the Wyse stepped back knowing the commissioning was done.

■ ■ ■

Charlie awoke in his bed wearing the same clothes from the day before. He felt recharged and alert. Something in him had changed. There was a power in him that was not there before. He sat up in his bed and recalled the dream he just had. Charlie could not remember seeing much except a bright light, but he couldn't shake the feeling of the dream. It was incredible! Never before had he felt so much power, contentment, and passion! Charlie had changed, and there was no going back!

XII

Ice Voyage

Wenzel was already on board by the time Charlie came to where the ship was docked. It was a huge dark ship with masts so tall they seemed to touch the clouds. The crew was so busy at work preparing the ship for departure, nobody paid much attention to Charlie standing staring at it. The captain of the ship, the Wyse of the Lonely Manor, was also busy in his cabin studying his charts.

Throwing his backpack over both shoulders, Charlie decided to start climbing up the rope ladder from the row boat. He was thankful he recently climbed up the tree outside his bedroom window in Howell to refresh his muscles on what to do. *Wow, that seemed so long ago,* he thought to himself. Once aboard the ship, he was greeted by the first-mate and shown to his quarters. Wenzel was already down in the hull of the ship. They were given a small space to share in a corner of the hold. Two cots were set up as well as two small lockers for their belongings. "Hey," Charlie said, greeting Wenzel.

"Hello, did you sleep well?" Wenzel asked wondering if Charlie felt the same as he did.

"Actually, I did! I feel so different. I feel like I have a new power inside me and that I am exactly where I am supposed to be!" Charlie responded enthusiastically.

"I have much the same feelings, Charlie. Whatever flowed through us last night was good, really good," Wenzel said with excitement in his voice.

"What do you know about the Presence?" Charlie asked.

"Not much. My aunt and uncle rarely spoke of it. Now and again they would refer to it for help. They never taught me about it though," Wenzel explained wishing he had paid more attention when he had the chance.

"I bet we will learn a lot more about it at the Lonely Manor. I thought I was done with school for the summer! I guess not," Charlie laughed out loud.

"What do you mean?" Wenzel asked.

"Oh, it's just that before I crawled through the tunnel that led me here, I was on vacation with my mom. My school had ended for the year, and I had two months off. Nothing has happened the way I expected it to happen," Charlie said trailing off suddenly feeling his former enthusiasm slip away.

Noticing Charlie's discomfort, Wenzel replied, "Cheer up, Charlie. I suspect that we will have the best adventure of our lives here. Nothing's happened as I anticipated either. Nothing ever went wrong in the Village of the Hill. It had been peaceful its whole existence until the Great Oak began to die. Part of me wants to be terrified."

"If I start to think about it long enough, I am scared too," Charlie said lying back on his cot. The two of them sat in silence for a while until a horn blew on the deck of the ship. Charlie and Wenzel jumped up and ran to see what was going on.

On the deck of the ship, all the crew were lined up facing the Captain's quarters. Outside the door, the Wyse of the Lonely Manor stood holding a shofar just like the one the Wyse of the Hill had, except his was slate colored. "Good morning, men," the Wyse began, "Today begins our most important journey in history. We are transporting the chosen ones to the safety of the Lonely Manor until they are ready for battle. Darkness is at work, so expect complications, be on guard, and like a wild dog drinking at a river, never let your ears down!" With that, he blew the shofar again, this time it was so loud it startled the crew. Wenzel and Charlie were a little nervous before, but after that speech, their previous confidence was shaken. They had no choice but to sail into the unknown.

■ ■ ■

Time on the ship passed without any major complications. Charlie had finally gotten over seasickness, and Wenzel had perfected his sea legs. Wenzel spent the bulk of the past two weeks shadowing the crew, learning everything he could. He had never been aboard a ship before and was curious about everything. Charlie, on the other hand, spent most of his time vomiting over the side of the ship trying to focus on the horizon as much as possible. He used to canoe and jet ski on Lake Thompson, but this was a whole different story! Finally, his equilibrium adjusted to the moving ship, and he was able to get to know the crew. The first mate was a man by the name of Henry. He was of average height and lean build. His face was both gentle and strong. Henry was respected by the crew, and it was probably because he showed kindness and fairness to them. His relationship with the Captain was good, too. Henry respected the Captain and believed in him one hundred percent. He was as loyal as loyal gets.

Then there was the cook, Skins. Charlie could not tell much about him. He was a quiet man about five inches shorter than Henry and about twenty pounds heavier. He did his job well but showed little interest in talking to anyone. Once Charlie caught a glimpse of a tattoo on his back. Skins was reaching for a sack of flour on a high shelf when his shirt lifted just enough for Charlie to make out a scaly leg with claws across his lower back. As soon as Skins noticed Charlie watching, he pulled down his shirt and snorted away. Charlie tried to apologize for staring, but it was too late.

The days passed slowly for Charlie. There was so much work to do on the ship. He helped when possible but worry about the future and about his mother whom he left behind, consumed him. Once in a while he would reflect back on the commissioning ceremony and the worry would ease, but he felt so unprepared. The biggest fight he had ever had was with his mother before they left for England. How could he possibly fight in a war against darkness?

That night at supper, Charlie sat next to Wenzel. "Feeling better, I see," Wenzel stated.

"Yes, I am. Finally!" Charlie said relieved.

"Isn't being on the ship great? I simply love working with the crew. My aunt and uncle would be so proud. They must be worried sick, though. I never had a chance to tell them I was leaving. In fact, I snuck out the last night I was with them," Wenzel admitted.

"The night you followed Mr. Littleston?"

"Yes, I knew they wouldn't have approved, but I went anyway. I just knew Mr. Littleston was the reason the Great Oak was dying. He had changed so much. He became obsessed with something. I was sure I'd discover it and save the tree if I followed him. I guess I was too late," Wenzel said with sadness in his eyes.

"Were you friends with him?" Charlie asked.

"I guess so. He lived down the road from us, and growing up I'd go and help him on his farm every day. He was so kind to me. Then one day I went to help. I hadn't been to see him in a while, and he shouted at me to leave his property. I stood there in shock, so he grabbed a broom and chased me down the road. Originally, I thought he was angry with me because I no longer helped him every day like I did as a boy. But the next day I was sitting under the Great Oak and saw the ugliest bird land on a branch. When it flew..."

"...away the branch died," Charlie interrupted.

"Yes, how did you know?" Wenzel asked confused.

Leaning in to whisper, Charlie said, "I found a book at my uncle's house and when I opened it, I read about you and the Great Oak. Whatever that book is, it really wanted me to meet you."

"I don't know about you, but I have a lot more questions than answers," Wenzel replied.

"Me, too," Charlie agreed.

That night, for the first time since they set sail, the sky was completely cloudless and millions of bright stars could be seen from the deck of the boat. The entire crew sat on deck staring at the majestic sky. The sea was perfectly calm, and it was the first time since aboard the ship, Charlie found himself truly enjoying it.

"Have you ever seen anything like it?" Wenzel asked in amazement.

"No, not in all my life!" Charlie exclaimed. Charlie lay down to better view the stars and before he knew it, he fell asleep to the gentle motion of the ship.

Unaware he had fallen asleep, Charlie began to dream. In his dream, he was still star-gazing with the crew. It was calm just as it had really been, but then something strange began to happen. The ship sailed into an unforeseen cold front. As soon as the bow of the ship entered the cold front, it began to freeze! Thick ice crawled over the ship covering every surface and person. It crackled loudly as the thick ice formed. Charlie stood up in shock watching as everything and everyone froze in place around him. His breath created eerie clouds as he watched in disbelief. He became so cold it hurt! The ship creaked in the silence. The once majestic sky had turned cloudy and hid the bright moon from view. Charlie slowly walked around the ship examining the iced-over crew. Wenzel was frozen in place gazing up at the sky. His eyes were still open. Henry was frozen leaning against a pole with his arms crossed. They looked eerily peaceful.

Charlie made his way to the Captain's quarters and forced open the frozen door. Inside at his desk, the Captain sat frozen and hunched over something. The room, too, was thickly covered in ice. It felt so uninviting and spooky. Charlie stepped closer and saw a shocking sight! It was his book that he found in Uncle Ralph's attic! With his heart pounding, and his breath clouding the view, Charlie stepped toward the book. He grabbed it off the desk and sat with a crunch on the Captain's bed. Lifting the face of the clock on the book, Charlie unlatched it. He opened the book and there on the first page was his name! Before he could read any further, Charlie heard something move outside the door. Quickly he re-latched the book and hid under the bed to avoid being seen by whatever or whomever was out there! A few seconds passed without any more movement. Then he saw it! A man's boots passed by the door. This time they stopped and someone turned to enter the Captain's room!

Charlie's heart beat out of his chest. The boots slowly walked across the room. Each step crunched loudly on the ice, making him even more anxious. The boots stopped at the Captain's desk. He heard shuffling as if someone was looking for something. Then he realized he had what the intruder was looking for! Hugging the book tightly, Charlie squeezed his eyes shut in an effort to disappear. He so badly wanted to be invisible. The shuffling stopped, and the boots quickly turned around. Charlie stopped breathing!

What seemed like hours passed by until the boots finally walked out. Terrified of moving, he stayed under the bed and fell asleep.

Suddenly, Charlie sprang up from where he was sitting watching the stars on the deck, still feeling the chill of his dream. In fact, his clothes had a small layer of ice on them! *What had just happened?* He thought to himself. Looking around, he discovered that everyone else had gone to bed. As Charlie stood up, something heavy fell off his lap and landed on his feet. Trying not to shout, he bent down and picked up what fell. It was his book! immediately, Charlie shoved it under his shirt and ran to his cot hoping no one saw him with it. How did it get out of his backpack in the locker? He now knew he wasn't the only one aware of this book. Someone on this ship was trying to steal it!

XIII

Malek

Charlie was anxiously waiting till it was safe to read the book again. With someone else on the ship looking for it, he couldn't be too careful! He had been hiding it under a loose board behind his locker since the dream. After navigating around storms and avoiding other ships, due to the secret nature of their journey, they finally arrived. Now that they had docked, it would soon be safe to read again. He would even be able to show it to Wenzel, he hoped.

Waiting on the shore for them was an entourage of black carriages drawn by giant Belgian horses. Servants were standing by, waiting to unload the ship with their row boats. Behind them were huge rolling green hills, and behind those hills were gigantic snow-peaked mountains that seemed to go on forever. Henry and the crew spent most of the morning tossing cargo to one another and lowering it down to the boats. Separate boats were set aside for passengers. The boat for Wenzel and Charlie was accompanied by armed guards wearing robes and swords. Wenzel and Charlie looked at each other in surprise! Things were getting more serious on every leg of the trip.

The carriage that was to take them to the Lonely Manor was also accompanied by armed guards. They were beginning to wonder if they were ever going to have time to talk in private. Before the land journey started, the Wyse of the Lonely Manor sent his servants to blindfold everyone. After everyone was blindfolded, the servants brought a warm bitter tea for everyone to drink. Charlie and Wenzel forced it down without arguing. It was strange and made them a little dizzy. The path to the Manor was highly secretive and only trusted to those who had sworn in blood to uphold its secret. Everyone, except for the Wyse and the guards, was blindfolded and given the bitter tea.

The journey lasted several hours with lots of winding roads. So much so, that Wenzel could not even keep track of the direction they were headed. For a while, he was sure they were heading north, but soon he couldn't tell if they were headed east or west. Without warning, the bitter tea took its effect, and both Charlie and Wenzel drifted off into a deep sleep.

By sunset, they all arrived at the Manor. The carriages stopped and the servants diligently came around to remove everyone's blindfolds and wake them up. What they opened their eyes to was impressive! Completely surrounded by tall snow-peaked mountains, there was no visible way in or out. The Manor itself was gray stone, ten stories tall. It was a large square with tall towers at each corner. In the center, was a very large courtyard, and in the middle of the that was a huge statue of the Wyse.

Wenzel and Charlie were quickly escorted to their rooms by the guards. Once in their rooms, the guards looked around for any suspicious things that might have changed since the room was prepared for them. They couldn't be too careful. Then they left, finally! Now it was Charlie's chance to talk!

"I've been keeping something from you, and now I can finally show it to you," Charlie said to Wenzel, pulling off his backpack.

Confused, Wenzel stepped close to Charlie, looked around to make sure no one was listening, and whispered, "What are you talking about?"

Instead of responding, Charlie removed the book from his backpack and placed it in Wenzel's hands. Wenzel examined the book curiously for a minute, then glanced up at Charlie with an inquisitive look. Charlie explained his ice dream experience, how someone else on the ship was looking for it, and how he didn't feel safe until now to tell him that he brought it with him from his Uncle Ralph's house.

"Let's open it," Charlie eagerly suggested, barely able to contain his excitement.

Wenzel hesitated, "Are you sure it's safe? Whoever was looking for it on the ship is here, too. Everyone on the ship came to the Manor."

"Maybe it will give us answers," Charlie suggested, shrugging his shoulders.

Feeling extremely curious and wanting some answers, Wenzel reluctantly agreed. Charlie lifted the face of the clock and unlatched the book. Inside they read:

"A heart that has been stone cold for hundreds of years is not easily softened. In all of history there has never been anyone like him. Immortalized by hate, he plagues the Land of Arar. Here is the story of MALEK." Wide eyed, Charlie and Wenzel looked up at each other, each thinking the same thing. Then they continued reading.

"Malek was born to a young couple deeply in love. Only married a year, his mother gave birth to twins, Malek and his twin sister Maleka. From an early age Malek was tormented with grief. At three years old, he horrifically watched from shore as his father's boat capsized, trapping the entire crew underneath. Devastated, his mother promised herself she would raise the twins the best she could. She worked very long hours to keep food on the table. She loved her children, and they deeply returned her affection. Every night their mother would open the musical locket given to her on her wedding day, and tell the children stories as they fell asleep. She'd tell stories of times long ago when kings and queens ruled and the land was at peace. The tales were always happy. The locket played a sweet melody so soft that it could soothe any hard feelings and wipe away the worries of the world. Young Malek loved listening to his mother sing along with the locket as he gazed into her eyes. To him, she was the most beautiful thing in the world!

Unfortunately, no locket could have kept him safe from the tragedy that lay ahead. The land he and his family lived in fell on hard times. Crops stopped growing even despite the abundant rainfall. At age eleven, on a dark stormy night, intruders burst through the door of their small home and kidnapped his mother and sister! The intruders sold his mother and sister into slavery, and Malek feared he'd never see them again.

Not knowing what to do, he devoted the rest of his life to finding them. After a few years of searching, he finally learned of their location! When he arrived at the plantation where they were sold to work hard laborious days, he was devastated to discover that the entire place had been set on fire! Searching through what he thought to be the slaves' homes, Malek found his mother's musical locket, untouched by the fire. From that day on, he vowed to find the people who did this to his family and make them pay!

Malek's loneliness grew deeper and with it, an immense bitterness towards joy. He began to hate his father for dying and not protecting his mother and sister. Hoping to find their killer, Malek at the age of 20, found a job as a deck hand on a slave transporting ship. The deep thirst for revenge kept him motivated and focused.

His first voyage on the slave transporting ship took him past the Land of the Beast. It was a luscious place that was uninhabited by humans because of the vicious beast the size of a mountain that lay sleeping on it. No ship had ever dared sail so close past it in fear of waking the beast. After witnessing his father's own horrible death and losing the rest of his family, revenge kept Malek unafraid of the creature. On the third week of the one-month-long voyage, Malek overheard the slave master brag about setting another slave master's plantation on fire because he had cheated him out of money. The master continued to say that everyone died, leaving nothing for any heirs. Malek's blood boiled! He was ready to avenge the death of his mother and sister immediately!

That night he convinced the slaves to overthrow the ship. So, as the slave master slept, the entire crew was tied up and thrown overboard! Malek's plan was genius! Now he was captain of a slave ship and was about to become a wealthy merchant. But, there were other forces at work. Just as the last man hit the water, a horrible storm overcame the sky. Thunder roared and rain pelted the deck. It was as if the sea became violently angry. The ship tossed back and forth between the waves like a wild animal trapped in a cage, finally crashing on the rocky shore! Twenty out of 150 slaves were instantly swallowed up by the ravenous sea. The rest of the slaves lay stranded, half-alive, on the shore of the Land of the Beast!

With morning came clear skies. From where they were shipwrecked, they could see the beast! No one had ever traveled near it before or dared to explore its land, and now the slaves and Malek were only a few miles from the creature's mouth! It was fierce looking. Its scales were jagged and rough. Its head was massive and crowned with sharp spear-like horns. It had the snout of a dragon, with teeth gleaming out from its closed jaw. The body was too big to see in its entirety. The head was supported by two blood-stained clawed feet. There was no doubt that at any moment, the beast could awaken and devour the entire group in one bite!

All that day, the slaves spent drying out and taking inventory of their losses. Anything that washed up on shore, they quickly gathered to a hidden area away from the Beast's view, in case it was to awaken. The next night on the island, the slaves and Malek slept huddled together to keep warm and safe. They were all cold, tired, and scared. Unsure what they were going to do or how they were to survive, they tried eagerly to sleep, but in the middle of the night, a bright white light flashed, awaking one of the slaves who went by the name Isaac. Not quite knowing where the light came from, he sat up startled and ready to defend himself. Then he saw it again! This time it looked like it came from the eye of the beast! It was waking up! Isaac was frightened and thought they were all in danger so he began to awaken the sleeping slave next to him just as he heard a voice. It was telling him to trust the Beast and everyone would be brought to safety.

Naturally being skeptical, Isaac thought dark magic was at play and plugged his ears to avoid further corruption, but then he heard the voice as clear as day inside his head! There was a pureness in the voice that made him trust it. He slowly unplugged his ears and sat contemplating quietly what to do next. At that, the wind suddenly picked up and blew away some sand to reveal a clay path. It was a winding path, but impossible to see when covered with sand. With confidence on what to do next, Isaac fell back asleep knowing where he was to lead the others.

The next morning there was a stirring of activity. The slaves were getting antsy, and they wanted off the beach. Isaac, feeling calm and controlled, woke up, shook the sand out of his hair, and explained that in the night he encountered a presence that would lead them to safety. He excitedly and full of hope showed them the path. Most of the slaves were also excited and eager to follow Isaac. Yet, there were others who opposed the idea, including Malek. "What do you mean there was a voice that told you to follow a path? Clearly, you are dehydrated and hallucinating!" mocked Malek. "Do you really expect us to follow a path that leads us closer to the Beast?!"

"You must trust me on this, Malek," Isaac reassured stepping closer to him, "I know in my mind that this is what we have to do to survive."

"Well, I saw a presence last night too," Malek lied haughtily taking a step towards Isaac and then turning around to corral the others, "and it showed me a different path. One that leads away from the Beast! Now, who will follow me?!"

There was an immediate uproar of shouts and arguing. Some slaves trusted Isaac in spite of what it looked like, but others were fearful and wanted to follow Malek. "Quiet!"

Isaac shouted trying to gain control, "Listen to me, everyone! We all want off this beach! Now we can either argue ourselves to death, or we can take action. All of you who want to go with me, step over here, and those who want to go with Malek stand by him." At that, the group was split in half and each group hastily went their separate ways.

For Isaac and his friends, the walk was easy despite the fact they had just been shipwrecked and were surrounded by sand. The clay path provided cool relief to their tired feet. Though they were headed toward the Beast, they were protected by the shade of the luscious fruit trees, and their days always ended by a refreshing water source. Each night, Isaac was awakened by the pure light, and each night a new clay path was exposed. Daily they came closer to the beast, and daily they trusted in the Presence more and more. Either they were being hypnotized by the Beast and being lured in to be devoured, or there was something outstandingly special about the creature. They wouldn't know for sure until they reached it.

On the fourth night Isaac was awakened, the clay path was revealed, and then the voice gave him a message, "Follow the path without hesitation. I will meet you there." In the morning, Isaac and the other slaves saw the path leading right into the Beast's now opened mouth! The other slaves began to question what was happening. Perhaps the voice was going to sacrifice them to the slumbering Beast! Calming the group down, Isaac reassured them the

Presence took care of them this far, and it will take care of them at the mouth of the Beast too. Isaac just knew it had to be true!

Malek and his followers headed as far from the Beast as they could. Their spirits were high knowing they were safe from the belly of the Beast. Each night, Malek awoke and swept a path to fool the others. The next morning he would tell his followers that a voice led him to a new path. Each day lying became easier for him and more convincing to the others. On the fifth day, the shaded trees turned into tangled jungle, and they became surrounded by stinky bogs. Bugs of all shapes and sizes fed off of them, and fresh food and water became scarce. Only the food that they had salvaged from the washed up shipwreck was keeping them alive.

Sensing the uneasiness of the group, Malek reassured them, "You are being tested. Just because it is hard and uncomfortable does not mean anything. The voice wants to know if you really trust him! Now is your chance. Stay with me or run to the mouth of the Beast." At that, Malek pointed to the creature. They could see the Beast's mouth perfectly from a large opening in the trees. They watched in horror as Isaac and his people willingly entered into the fang-lined mouth! A bright light flashed over the island and the ground shook knocking Malek and the other slaves down. They began to shout in fear and confusion! What was happening? What would happen to them? "Silence!

Silence!" Malek shouted, "We must push on. We are getting close and soon will be far far away from that vicious creature." Without hesitation, the group journeyed deeper into the dark swampy jungle.

But that night, Malek couldn't sleep. The image of Isaac and the others entering the Beast's mouth played over and over in his head. Malek grew angrier and angrier each time he thought about it. Then, a voice spoke to him,"You have chosen this path for yourself," it said. "Your selfishness and bitterness have brought you to this dark place. Here you will stay until you are no longer full of hate. You cannot enter the protection of the Beast with a hardened heart." Malek burned with even more anger! Out of control, he grabbed a large rock and threw it with all his strength towards the voice, but the rock crushed a slave's head, killing him instantly! Immediately, the others woke up. There was an uproar of confusion and blame. Malek pretended to have just awakened too and walked over to the dead slave pretending to be shocked.

"Who did this?" he said accusingly. No one admitted to it. "Confess!" He shouted louder. Still burning with anger from what the voice said to him, Malek searched through the crowd and found an ugly looking man. "It was you! Confess or I will put you to death for treason!" The man was outraged by the accusation and denied it immediately. Without hesitation, Malek picked up the same rock that had just killed the slave and killed the man too. The people

gasped in disbelief and fear. "We can't have a murderer among us," Malek nervously explained, "Now go back to bed! We move in the morning."

Wenzel and Charlie stood looking at each other in disbelief, but before they could say anything, someone loudly knocked on their door three times causing both of them to jump. Charlie quickly stuffed the book under his shirt right as the door opened.

XIV

Skins Disappears

The door swung open and five armed guards burst in with their swords drawn. They searched the room tipping over furniture in a hurry. "He's not here," one shouted signaling to move on, and all the guards ran out of the room.

"Come on! Let's see what's going on," Wenzel said as he ran out the door. Making sure the book was securely under his shirt, Charlie quickly followed after Wenzel.

■ ■ ■

Skins snuck away and made his way to the edge of the mountain range that encircled the Lonely Manor. Knowing he was safe if unseen, he crawled under a pine tree and covered himself in fallen needles to keep warm as he slept. If he could lie low for awhile without getting caught, his plan would work! By morning his skin was itchy, and the necklace chain around his neck was burning red hot. It was beginning to happen! If it happened too soon, then he would run the risk of being discovered. This had to work! It just had to! There were no more options. Failure meant death!

■ ■ ■

The Wyse of the Lonely Manor spent the entire night pacing in his room. The book was missing and so was Skins. All the other men were accounted for. The Wyse had been suspicious of Skins the moment he saw his face. There was something a little too convenient about how they met. His original cook suddenly got ill and died right before the previous voyage. Then, when he went to tell Henry about the need to hire a new cook, he saw Skins standing next to Henry asking for a job. At first, the Wyse had pity on the sad-looking man, and thus hired on the spot. But, as time passed on the voyage, he began to suspect Skins of darkness. Skins didn't speak with any of the other crew. He kept himself busy, and once in a while the Wyse heard Skins whispering to himself. He was uncomfortably secretive, and now, with both the book and Skins missing, he was sure of it! Skins was a spy for Malek!

The next morning, Charlie and Wenzel got up, securely hid the book in some loose floor boards under one of the beds, and then ran to the courtyard to see what was going on. Everyone else was gathered there and looking panicked. The Wyse of the Lonely Manor was front and center. "Quiet! Quiet! I need everyone to calm down and listen carefully." The crowd calmed down and gave the Wyse their full attention. "I have good reason to believe that Skins is a traitor. If anyone finds him, they are to bring him to me immediately, or else you, too, will become a traitor. Darkness has crept into the Hill and now, I fear, it threatens us! The Lonely Manor has been a sanctuary to allies of the Presence for centuries. Skins may have jeopardized this! Anyone having any information is to report to me immediately." With that, the Wyse quickly spun around and hurriedly walked back inside.

"Did you see that?" Wenzel asked.

"See what?" Charlie asked feeling confused.

"The Wyse. His face was covered in worry, and after reading about what Malek is capable of, I'm worried too," Wenzel admitted.

"Yay, that makes three of us. Somehow, you and I are supposed to stop this," Charlie said doubting the meaning of his words.

The entire Manor was on lockdown. No one could go in or out except the guards and the Wyse. Guards were posted on each tower of the Manor. Charlie and Wenzel felt more like they were in a prison than a sanctuary. Either way, with the distraction Skins had made, Charlie and Wenzel could finally relax in privacy. Their training was postponed for at least a few more days.

After a good night's rest, Charlie woke up with a spring in his step! He was ready to explore the Manor! The day was bright and warm, and despite the surrounding circumstances, Charlie was determined to have some fun. The birds were singing and big fluffy clouds danced across the blue sky. Charlie looked over at Wenzel's bed, but he was not there. After quickly getting dressed, Charlie checked to make sure the book was safe, then made his way down to the dining hall. All the walls were built from giant gray stones.

Tapestries of many colors and large paintings brought life to the otherwise dull walls. Intricate details carved in the stone decorated windows and doorways. Signs, too, were carved directly into the walls, which Charlie was grateful for or else he would get very lost!

As he approached the dining hall, the most delicious smells floated through the hallway to meet him. Once he entered, his eyes were even more pleasantly surprised. The dining hall had four long rectangular tables with benches on either side. It looked like it could seat about 400 people. At the front of the dining hall, smaller tables lined the wall. Each table was filled with fresh foods. One was of warm waffles, pancakes, pastries, and muffins. Another table gleamed with sparkling fresh fruit. Apples, bananas, oranges, strawberries, blueberries, raspberries, kiwi, pineapple, and several odd-shaped fruits he had never seen before deliciously tempted him! It was incredible! Huge fountains of milk and juice were perfectly placed in the center of all the tables. Another table yet was filled with hot meat and eggs. Charlie hadn't realized how hungry he was until then. His stomach growled so loudly that he was sure the people standing near him heard it. Not hesitating any longer, Charlie filled a plate, found a seat, and began to devour his scrumptious breakfast.

With a full belly, Charlie remembered he still hadn't seen Wenzel. Grabbing one more delicious-looking pastry on his way out, he decided to continue looking for his friend. Charlie stopped by their room one more time to see if Wenzel had returned. He hadn't. So instead, Charlie grabbed the book and hid it under his shirt, just in case someone would decide to search for it again.

Having explored most of the east side of the Manor the night before, he decided to head to the south side of the Manor. On his way, he saw signs for the library, the greenhouse, the washing room, the sitting room, the lounging room, the formal hall, the servant's quarters, and even the attic. *Wow! There is so much to explore!* Charlie thought to himself. Finally, he came to the end of the hall. There was a grand wooden door carved with beautiful nature scenes.

He stood admiring the door when he began to hear strange whispering. Thinking it was coming from the other side of the door, he pressed his ear against it and listened. The door was too thick. There was no way the voices were coming through it. He stood in front of the door and waited to hear it again. He did! This time he could tell that the noise was coming from a crack in the wall just to the left of the door. Charlie pressed his ear against the crack to listen, but instead of hearing something, a small hidden passage-way pushed open! Nearly falling in, he caught his step and began slowing walking inside. The door quickly slammed shut behind him leaving him in total darkness. Then, he heard the whispering again! Feeling around with his hands, he followed the voices down a short hallway until he came to another wall with a crack. This time he thought twice about leaning against it to listen. The voices were much easier to hear at this point. He could even make out who was talking. It was Wenzel and the Wyse!

Wanting to hear what they were saying, Charlie pressed his ear against the crack, and just like last time, the hidden door flung open knocking Charlie to the ground! Surprised, Charlie looked up in embarrassment. Wenzel and the Wyse stopped talking to each other and just stood staring at the clumsy Charlie on the floor. Then unable to hold it in, the Wyse broke out in wild laughter! He had been so tense about everything going on, this was just what he needed to release his anxiety. After a few minutes of everyone laughing, Wenzel helped Charlie off the floor. In doing so, the book that was hidden under Charlie's shirt fell and slid across the room to the Wyse's feet. Wenzel and Charlie froze in fear!

The Wyse's face changed from jolly to serious as he slowly bent down and picked up the book. "Where did you get this?" he asked sternly staring them both in the eyes. Charlie and Wenzel just stood there not quite sure how to explain it.

"I had a dream," Charlie began, "In my dream the whole ship and everybody on it were frozen. When I entered your cabin, I saw you hunched over this book. I found this book at my Aunt and Uncle's house and was curious as to why you had it. I picked it up to examine it. At the same time, I heard footsteps coming up the stairs towards your cabin. I hid under your bed. Someone came into your room to look for the book. From then on I have kept it hidden."

"Is that so?" the Wyse said as he turned to look out the window, his hands behind his back holding the book.

"I'm sorry, sir. I should have come to you sooner," Charlie apologized.

"I'm sorry too, sir. I knew about it as well," Wenzel admitted.

"Have you opened it?" the Wyse asked.

"Yes," both Charlie and Wenzel said together.

The Wyse did not say anything else. He walked across the study and sat down in a tall back chair, crossed his legs, placed the book on his legs, and folded his hands under his chin with his elbows resting on the arm rests.

"What did you learn?" he finally asked.

Wenzel jumped in to explain, "We learned about Malek's past and the foundation of the Hill."

"Very well," the Wyse said stoically, "The book only reveals things the reader needs to see. The Presence designed it that way. Take the book and keep it hidden. Tell no one else about it. It is better if everyone thinks it is missing. If it gets into the wrong hands, dark magic can force it to show things. Be on guard!"

Wenzel and Charlie stood there not knowing what to say. "Okay, sir," was all they felt was appropriate. The Wyse handed Charlie the book and nodded for them to leave, and they obeyed right away. Charlie stuffed the book back under his shirt. He was going to have to find a better way to hide it. He can't have it falling out like that again!

XV

A Lost Traveler

Things began to cool down at the Manor. Still, there was no sign of Skins, and the sense of security of the Lonely Manor returned. Everyone resumed to their normal routines, and the talk of Malek also died down. By now training for Charlie and Wenzel had been going on for several very long tedious days. The Wyse had been tutoring both Charlie and Wenzel in the history of the Hill and surrounding areas, military tactics, survival techniques, battle skills, and everything else that could possibly prepare them for the attacks Malek was preparing to make on the Hill and its allies. The days were long and exhausting. With winter approaching, the Wyse estimated they still had some time for solid training before Malek would full-on attack. Even so, it was uncertain whether it was going to be enough. It just had to be! There was no other choice. In fact, Wenzel and Charlie were the only choices.

Charlie sat down next to Wenzel in the dining hall. "I'm beat," Charlie said with exhaustion.

"Me, too," Wenzel replied.

"I've learned so much and trained so hard that even in my dreams I'm training!" Charlie admitted.

"Ha-ha," Wenzel snickered, "I've heard you talking in your sleep."

"There's the proof. I can't escape it!" Charlie said letting out a laugh.

"Look at it this way, you are double training," Wenzel said teasingly.

Before Wenzel could say another word, a huge bell rang through the Manor shaking the dishes on the table. The violent vibrations from the sound of the bell shook Charlie's fork off the table landing by his shoe. Wenzel and Charlie looked at each other with concern and curiosity. It rang again! And again! "Look!" someone shouted while pointing out the window. Charlie and Wenzel jumped up and ran to the window along with everyone else.

The sun was setting, and it was nearly completely dark. The wind howled through the valley and seemingly bounced off the surrounding mountains. The temperature had dropped drastically from earlier in the day, and it had begun to snow. Out in the distance, Charlie and Wenzel could barely make out a small figure hunched over walking slowly towards the Manor. The figure was dressed in a long cloak and looked to be barefoot. The guards, posted on all four towers with their bows and arrows drawn towards the unknown figure, waited for the Wyse of the Lonely Manor to give the signal to shoot. The bell continued to ring as other guards got into position on the ground.

After several minutes, Charlie and Wenzel could see the struggling figure more clearly. It looked like a girl! "What is a girl doing out here?" Wenzel exclaimed. Alarm set into Charlie and Wenzel. "Could this be an attack from Malek?" Wenzel whispered to Charlie.

"I don't know," Charlie replied, "Let's not wait to find out." Charlie and Wenzel ran back to their room and took out the book from under the loose floor board. With a quick glance at each other, Charlie flung it open and began to read:

It was a cold winter day. The snow was falling heavily on the Village. Trina paced the small cabin to ease her labor pains. William had just gone out to get the midwife. The baby was going to be born soon! Trina's heart filled with joy at the thought of finally meeting her baby! But it filled with sorrow knowing that in a few short months, she'd have to leave the baby behind to fulfill a duty. She pushed that thought aside as an intense contraction stole all her focus. If William didn't arrive soon, the baby would be born without the midwife! Trina continued to pace the floor, only stopping when heavy contractions forced her to.

Suddenly, the door flung open sending a gust of cold wind straight at Trina. She was relieved to see William and the midwife. It was time to push! William, too, was excited to meet his baby. He broke custom and decided to stay in the room to watch the child be born. He did not want to miss any more of this child's life than he had to. With three hard pushes, the baby was born. It was a healthy baby boy!

Charlie shut the book and looked confusingly at Wenzel. "What does it mean?" asked Charlie.

"I'm not sure . . . " Wenzel trailed off with an uneasy feeling in his gut.

Suddenly the warning bells rang out four times! Charlie quickly hid the book again and followed Wenzel back to the dining hall. When they arrived they could not believe their eyes! Five guards with swords drawn surrounded a small cloaked figure shivering on the ground. The Wyse of the Manor stood on a platform observing from a distance. Worry and concern filled his face with wrinkles. He suspected dark magic. Then he nodded to one of the guards. At once, the guard ripped off the cloak to reveal the suspicious traveler. Everyone gasped at the sight! It was a young woman not more than eighteen years of age with long dark tangled hair. Her feet were filthy and bright red from being exposed to the cold. Her clothes were dirty and torn. She looked like she had been lost for a long time wandering in the wilderness.

The Wyse jumped down off the platform and pushed his way through the crowd. He pushed two guards aside and stood staring in disbelief at the sight. *No one can accidentally come here! He thought. This Manor is protected by the Presence. Either it's dark magic or the Presence wanted her here.* As if hearing his thoughts, the girl lifted her head and looked helplessly into his eyes. She was pleading for help. Then she fainted from exhaustion. The guards lifted her up and took her to lie down under surveillance. "Make sure she gets a hot meal, a warm bath, and clean clothes. I want her to be ready to talk when I come," the Wyse demanded. The head guard nodded and went off to do exactly as he was told.

The Wyse just stood staring at the floor where the strange girl once lay. A million thoughts raced through his head. Charlie and Wenzel stood helplessly staring at the Wyse. They knew that if he was worried then they, too, should be worried.

XVI

Mr. Ignas

Charlie and Wenzel stood waiting for the Wyse to arrive near the fountain in the courtyard for their next day of training. It was unlike the Wyse to be late. Charlie sat on the wall of the fountain splashing a stick in the water. Wenzel paced back and forth in front of the fountain kicking a small rock as he went. They were anxious to ask the Wyse about the strange girl. The sound of footsteps stopped both of them and caused them to look towards the sound. It took a few more seconds before they saw a short-statured man wearing a brown three-piece suit, brown patent leather shoes, and a brown rimmed hat. The man walked swiftly and straight at Wenzel and Charlie. He abruptly stopped in front of the two and said, "Good morning, young men. Today I will be training you in survival. My name is Mr. Ignas. The Wyse has sent me. He is occupied for the rest of the day. You understand," Mr. Ignas said with a nod and stuck out his hand to shake Wenzel's, then Charlie's. "This way please," he said without any further explanation or delay.

Charlie tossed down his stick and jumped from the wall. Wenzel followed Charlie as they both walked quickly to catch up. Mr. Ignas never looked back. He walked to the south side of the Manor and stopped at a small black door. He pulled an old key out of his pocket and unlocked it. Wenzel glanced at Charlie with a shrug. They were nervous to leave the Manor. With everything that had just happened, they preferred to stay within the security of its walls.

Without hesitation, Mr. Ignas motioned the boys to pass through the door. He locked it behind them and continued on just as fast as before. They followed a little dirt path no wider than a man's foot. The path curved around to the north side of the building where three horses were saddled and waiting for them. Mr. Ignas abruptly stopped and turned to face the two boys. "Have you ever ridden a horse?" Mr. Ignas asked very matter of factly.

"Yes, sir," Wenzel said confidently.

"Only a pony when I was four, sir," replied Charlie sheepishly. Wenzel began to laugh but stopped when Charlie's elbow told him he should.

"Very well," Mr. Ignas said stoically. "It is simple. Sit on the horse. Don't make the horse mad. Don't fall off. Are you ready?"

"Ready," said Wenzel who was already mounted on the horse.

"Ready," said Charlie with a hard lump in his throat. He clumsily pulled himself up. Mr. Ignas watched him from on top of his own horse.

Once Charlie was on, Mr. Ignas took off! Wenzel quickly followed. Charlie, not wanting to be left behind, and having the feeling that no one was going to wait for him, mimicked them and took off too.

They rode for thirty minutes and stopped next to a beautiful waterfall in the woods. It was a refreshing sight. Mr. Ignas and Wenzel gracefully dismounted. Charlie tried to dismount, but his right foot got stuck in the holster causing him to fall. Once again, Wenzel began to chuckle. Charlie shot him a look, and Wenzel stopped immediately by biting his lip. Attempting to salvage any dignity left, Charlie stood up and dusted himself off trying not to look embarrassed.

Without saying a word, Mr. Ignas knelt down and began brushing the ground searching for something. The boys stood watching. Mr. Ignas grabbed two rocks and stuck them in his pocket. He went over to a tree and began collecting dry grass and weeds. He walked over to a clear flat area and placed the dry grass in a loose small pile. He then walked over to a tree and collected small twigs and thin sticks. He placed them near the grass pile. He walked over to a fallen tree and gathered larger branches and dry logs placing them near the other piles. Mr. Ignas then took the two stones out of his pocket, knelt down next to the grass, and began hitting the stones together. After three strikes, a big spark leapt onto the pile of grass and weeds. Quickly, Mr. Ignas dropped the stones and began blowing the grass pile to keep it ablaze. Once it was good and burning, he began adding the small twigs and sticks to the fire. After a couple more minutes, he added the large branches and had a beautiful roaring fire. Mr. Ignas looked up at Charlie and Wenzel and said, "Now you do it," and sat down on a rock near his fire.

Charlie and Wenzel looked at each other comically but realized it wasn't a joke. They got to work immediately. Quickly, they gathered everything they needed, including the two pieces of flint rock to strike together. They spent the rest of the day trying to start their fires. First, it took them thirty minutes to get a good enough spark to start their grass pile on fire. But they didn't blow on it enough, and it died before they could place the twigs on it. Then they blew on it enough but smothered it with twigs. They both even got far enough to start placing large branches on their fires, but both boys choose partially wet logs so their fires died down quickly.

They were hot, sweating, dirty, and exhausted. All the while, Mr. Ignas said nothing. He just sat watching them carefully. Finally, as the sun was beginning to set and with stomachs rumbling, Charlie and Wenzel accomplished two roaring fires! Mr. Ignas reached behind the rock he was sitting on and pulled up a brown canvas sack. Inside was water (which the boys chugged immediately), biscuit batter, and vegetables. Mr. Ignas gave the food to the boys and said, "If you can cook it, you can eat it."

Without saying a word, Wenzel and Charlie went to work looking for ways to cook the food. Wenzel found a thin flat rock wide enough to place food on top. He put the rock in the fire and let it heat up as he prepared the vegetables. Mr. Ignas was kind enough to supply a knife. When the stone was nice and hot, Wenzel dropped dollops of batter on the rock. It sizzled like music to the hungry boys' ears. Wenzel placed the vegetables next to the biscuits and used the knife to flip his food. Charlie took a different approach. He found some wide leaves to wrap his food in. One leaf contained the batter, and a second leaf contained the vegetables. Using his shoe laces, he tied the leaves to the end of a long stick and dangled the food above the fire. The moisture in the leaves steamed the vegetables and biscuit batter. Charlie and Wenzel were so busy cooking and eating that they failed to notice Mr. Ignas cooking with a pot and utensils.

After everyone's bellies were satisfied, Mr. Ignas jumped in with a question. "What did you learn today, boys?"

After a few seconds of awkward silence as the boys finished chewing the huge bites of food they had just stuffed in their mouths, Charlie answered, "How to build a fire from things found in nature."

"Wrong!" Mr. Ignas blurted out while pointing his knife with a biscuit on the end at Charlie. A few minutes of silence went by before he said, "A deeper lesson of survival was taught today, and you failed."

With a lump in his throat, Wenzel bravely spoke up, "What do you mean, sir?"

"Survival is about using any resource available to get a task done as quickly and safely as possible. You spent all day building one fire and only ate one meal. Neither of you used the greatest resource you had . . . me."

Without anything further to say, Mr. Ignas signaled the boys to quickly finish their food and clean up. They rode back to the Manor in silence, each boy deeply considering what they had learned. It was dark and the path was only lit by moonlight, but they all managed to stay together.

Back at their room, Charlie and Wenzel collapsed on their beds from physical and mental exhaustion. Both were too tired to talk to each other, and besides, they had a lot to process about today's training with Mr. Ignas.

XVII

The New Student

Five guards were stationed outside the door, and six guards were stationed inside. One of the girl's feet was tethered to the bed frame. She had been allowed a private bath and was provided with clean clothes. The only thing that remained on her from before was a dark colored gem necklace. While finishing a hot bowl of porridge, the Wyse stormed into the room slamming the door behind him. The sound of the door startled the girl causing the bowl to drop and the rest of her porridge to spill all over the floor. Holding back tears, she looked at him helplessly as he towered over her. "Who ARE you?!" The Wyse demanded forcefully.

"My name is Muriphany," she said nervously.

"How did you get here?" The Wyse demanded again.

"I walked," she quietly replied looking at the ground.

"I KNOW you walked, but how did you come to find this place? Its borders are hidden and protected. No one can just come walking in!" He shouted. The Wyse was burning with anger and suspicion. With Malek attacking the Hill, there was no room for politeness. Answers had to be found!

"I . . .I . . .don't know," she said, then began to cry.

Feeling annoyed by her weakness, he ordered the guards to only give her water for the rest of the day.

The Wyse stormed back to his study and locked himself in. He needed time to think. *Maybe I missed something? What am I not seeing? h*e thought. He paced his study for an hour. Occasionally, he stopped to stare out the window hoping for some hidden evidence to surface before his eyes. Nothing. Then he remembered the old scrolls in the library. Not wanting to run into anybody, he took the secret passageway through the walls. When he arrived in the library, he was relieved to see no one else there. Quickly, he made his way to where the scrolls were kept under lock and key. These scrolls dated back further than the foundation of the Hill. The Wyse rummaged around for a few minutes until he found it: "Hidden Manor." He stuffed it under his jacket and made his way back to his study through the hidden passages in the walls. Drawing all the curtains tightly shut and lighting a candle at his desk, he pulled the scroll out and carefully unrolled it. He did not want to risk anyone else reading this scroll!

■ ■ ■

Meanwhile, Charlie and Wenzel were with Mr. Ignas. Their lesson was less physically draining this time. Mr. Ignas spent the entire morning telling them stories of travel. He talked about how to go through cities without being noticed, how to bargain and trade with farmers for food, and what to do when confronted with opposition. Wenzel and Charlie's hands ached from taking notes so quickly. Charlie felt like he was back in Mr. Orangelo's class when time was standing still! Finally. Mr. Ignas gave them a ten-minute break. Charlie immediately stood up to stretch his legs. Wenzel sat thinking for a few minutes before he got up and made his way to the window. "Are you okay?" Charlie asked.

"Yes, just thinking," Wenzel quietly replied without making eye contact.

"What are you thinking about?" Charlie prodded.

"Um, nothing," he said shrugging it off, not wanting Charlie to ask any more questions.

They stood in awkward silence for a few minutes until Charlie said,

"Today's lesson is a lesson in time travel."

"What do you mean?" Wenzel asked inquisitively.

"Mr. Ignas is teaching us that time really does stand still!" Charlie said with a laugh. His joke was just enough to break the tension, and Wenzel began to laugh too. Just then, Mr. Ignas returned and resumed his lecture.

"The next lesson I am going to share with you is a lesson on unexpected things. Out there, beyond the Manor's property, lies danger far beyond any you could ever imagine. Things that appear safe can be a trap, and danger can turn into your best ally. Never trust your feelings alone. Always test them against the three harbor lights. For example, in the harbor you entered to begin your hidden journey to this place, there were three light towers that burned brightly to guide ships in at night. If when entering, all three lights lined up, you were safe to pass, but if they were not lined up, then you would surely crash on the hidden rocks below the surface. So the three harbor lights that I want you to remember are these: 1. Do your Allies agree with you? 2. Do you have a peace in your heart and mind about it? And 3. Does it line up with the teachings of the Presence given to you through the Wyse? If you can answer yes to all three of these questions, then it is a good choice. But be cautious and stay on your toes! Just as a wild dog refreshes at the pool with his ears up, always watch for danger. Never let your guard down, even when you think you are safe."

Just then, a bell rang out through the whole Manor. Mr. Ignas jumped to his feet and urged the boys to follow immediately. Wenzel and Charlie did not hesitate and quickly followed him into the dining hall. Everyone in the entire Manor was there. The Wyse paced the platform waiting impatiently for everyone to arrive. "As of recent," he began, "we have a new guest with us." His face showed little expression. Charlie and Wenzel could not tell whether the Wyse was happy or upset about it. "I want you to meet her, and welcome her to the Manor. She is going to study alongside Wenzel and Charlie." Charlie and Wenzel glanced at each other unsure how to take the news. The Wyse continued, "Her name is Muriphany and here she is!" At that, two guards escorted her onto the platform as everyone in the dining hall gave her a confused, half-hearted applause accompanied by gasping.

There she stood, a small framed, dark-haired, feeble-looking young woman. She looked nervous and unconfident. She wore a dark purple dress, and around her neck hung a dark red heptagon-shaped gem pendant. The thick gold chain contrasted with her delicate pale neck. It looked as if it were weighing her down. "You are dismissed," the Wyse said abruptly, then stormed off the stage. Muriphany looked nervously at the guards, unsure if they were going to allow her to leave the platform. One guard firmly grabbed her upper arm and escorted her roughly to Mr. Ignas.

Mr. Ignas looked at the boys and said, "Let us all continue," and walked away. Charlie, Wenzel, and now Muriphany looked at each other and quickly followed. Thoughts flooded Wenzel's head. *Where did she come from? How did she get here? Can we trust her? Is this a test?*

On guard, Wenzel took his seat next to Charlie. He couldn't wait to talk to him in private. For the rest of the class, Muriphany sat saying nothing and barely glanced up to look at any of them. She looked as if at any minute the wind would blow her over.

When class ended, Charlie and Wenzel raced to the dining hall eager to eat. Muriphany slowly followed behind them. In line, Charlie leaned over to Wenzel and whispered, "Do you think we should invite her to sit with us?"

Not sure how to respond, Wenzel replied, "Maybe we need to observe her a little more before we let her get close." Satisfied with that answer, Charlie found a seat where they could observe Muriphany at dinner. They watched her heap piles of food onto her plate. She weakly walked to an open table and began to wolf down her food.

Charlie and Wenzel were shocked to see such a dainty girl eat so much and so fast. When she finished, she got up and left the dining hall in a hurry. Charlie and Wenzel, surprised by her sudden urgency, jumped up and followed her. At first they thought she was going to her room to sleep off the massive amount of food she had just consumed, but she turned toward the stairwell instead. Charlie and Wenzel waited for her to begin up the stairs before they got any closer. Muriphany looked around to make sure she wasn't being watched and then darted up the stairs! Without hesitation, Charlie and Wenzel ran where she had been.

When they got there, they could only hear the echo of her shoes running up the stone steps. Knowing she'd hear them if they starting running up too, Charlie and Wenzel took their shoes off, and with shoes in hand, ran to catch up. It wasn't until the boys were at the third floor that they heard her shoes stop. With caution, they peaked around the corner before proceeding. They didn't see her, so they continued on till the next corner. At the fourth floor, they saw that a door was cracked open. With shoes still off, the boys crept toward the door and quietly peered in. At the end of a long corridor was a huge stained-glass octagon shaped window. Muriphany was standing gazing at it while holding the necklace that hung around her small neck. The boys stood watching her until she began to struggle with an unseen force and fainted! Immediately Wenzel and Charlie ran to her in worry.

She was still breathing and didn't appear to be hurt, but something was strangely wrong. Wenzel carefully lifted her up and quickly carried her down the stairs only stopping when Charle suggested they'd go faster if they put their shoes back on. They brought her to their room and laid her on one of the beds. Breathing heavily, Wenzel said, "Go get Mr. Ignas! He needs to know." With a nod, Charlie ran and found Mr. Ignas in the library rummaging through books. Sitting at a small table, he was nearly buried in tall stacks of books with several of them spread open.

"Come quick!" Charlie blurted.

Glancing up from his books, Mr. Ignas calmly closed the one he was reading and placed his reading glasses on top. "What is the emergency?" he asked.

"It's Muriphany. She's fainted!" Charlie said with a slight panic.

Suspiciously, Mr. Ignas replied, "Really?" He stood up and followed Charlie back to the room.

Upon arrival, Mr. Ignas immediately walked over to Muriphany and began to examine her closely but without touching her. She looked as if she was in a deep trance. He took a pencil out of his pocket and moved her hair away from her neck. "Hmmm," he said, "You see this, boys? That is peculiar." Wenzel and Charlie leaned in and saw it too! Around the back of her neck where the chain of the necklace touched her skin, was all black and blue as if she had been strangled! Mr. Ignas released her hair, put the pencil in his pocket, and quickly picked up Muriphany. "Follow me, and fast!" He commanded and dashed out the door. Charlie and Wenzel had to run to keep up with Mr. Ignas. He was strangely strong and fast for such a short nerdy-looking man. They couldn't tell where he was taking her. At first, they thought he was going to the Wyse, but instead of turning towards the Wyse's study, Mr. Ignas turned down a corridor the boys had never been before. Mr. Ignas flung open a door and continued running down another smaller hallway. To their left was a stone wall with a window to an outdoor stable, and to their right was the wall of a greenhouse. At the end of the hall, on the right, was a door into the greenhouse.

Mr. Ignas, once again, flung open the door and in one graceful swoop, used Muriphany's body to clear a table as he laid her on it. He locked the door behind them and then took off running deeper into the greenhouse. A few seconds later, Mr. Ignas ran back nearly dragging an older woman behind him. The woman was of medium stature. She was slightly pudgy and wore a modest dark green dress. Her completely gray hair was pulled up into a tidy bun except for a few curls that fell at her gently wrinkled face. Not saying a word and this time using his hand, Mr. Ignas pulled Muriphany's hair away from her neck exposing the bruises. The woman's eyes grew very big and she exclaimed, "Oh! Dear! I see why you have come!" Charlie and Wenzel just stood looking at each other and the woman. "Who knows of this?" The woman asked.

"Only us. Is that right, boys?"

"Yes, sir," Charlie and Wenzel said in unison.

"I have only read about this. I have never, in my wildest dreams, thought that I'd ever see this!" She said amazed, covering her mouth with one hand in disbelief.

"What is it?" Charlie boyishly asked.

"It is dark magic," the woman said gravely turning to face him. "Whatever this young lady has gotten herself into has its claws in her!"

"I recognized it right away and came as quickly as I could, Olive. I knew that if anyone could help her, it'd be you. Your knowledge far outreaches botany," Mr. Ignas acknowledged. "Can you help her?" He asked.

"I'm not sure," she said glaring at Muriphany with concern. "I will try," she said looking at Mr. Ignas with determination.

"Charlie, Wenzel, stay here with Professor Longtree. I am going to get the Wyse. It is important that no one else finds out! Understood?"

"Understood, sir," they said.

XVIII

The Cost of Betrayal

"Let me go!" Mr. Littleston screamed with agony. "Don't keep me here!" Malek paced back and forth in front of the cage he had stuffed the little coward into. He turned, bent down, made eye contact with Mr. Littleston, and evilly glared into his sad, pathetic eyes.

"Why would I keep you?" He snarled. "You mean nothing to me!" Malek stood up and stormed away in anger shouting to the guards, "Let him starve!"

"Noooooo! Noooo! You can't leave me here! I helped you! I gave you, Wenzel!" Mr. Littleston pleaded. Malek spun around in his tracks and darted toward the cage with rage. He reached in, grabbed Mr. Littleston by the neck, and growled in his face. With inhuman force, Malek threw Mr. Littleston to the ground causing him to smash his head on a rock. He was no more. Malek kicked the cage in anger and stormed away into the night.

XIX

Herbs and Ointments

As soon as Mr. Ignas left, Olive got to work. She dashed around her greenhouse collecting leaves, sap, and petals. Some were fresh and others were dry and hanging from the ceiling. With fervor, she began crushing and extracting liquids. Sweat poured down her brow as she worked. Within minutes, Mr. Ignas and the Wyse burst back into the greenhouse. Olive didn't look up but kept on working. The Wyse ran to Muriphany and immediately began examining her. Charlie and Wenzel watched in silence as the mystery unfolded in front of their eyes.

"I've never seen anything like this before," the Wyse said, concerned.

"What does it mean exactly?" Mr. Ignas asked.

"It means that she fought against dark magic and failed," he replied.

"Did we find her in time?" Wenzel jumped in feeling worried.

"Only Professor Longtree will be able to tell. We must let her work. In the meantime, stay here, Olive may need your help!" the Wyse exclaimed. Then the Wyse and Mr. Ignas left, leaving the three of them to tend to Muriphany.

Over the next several hours, Charlie and Wenzel sat watching as Professor Longtree scurried around the greenhouse. She applied herb concoctions to the bottoms of Muriphany's feet, back of the neck, and temples. She rubbed ointments on her wrists and sternum, all the while observing and recording Muriphany's breathing, pulse, and skin tone. Now and then, Professor Longtree barked a command at Charlie or Wenzel which they obeyed without question.

There was no time to be polite. Muriphany's life was at stake! As day turned into night, Muriphany's color turned from a pale whitish gray to a pale pink, her breathing steadied, and her pulse slowed down. "Light the lamps," Professor Longtree demanded as she entered the tool shed of her greenhouse. Wenzel jumped up and quickly lit the lamps before the last rays of the sunshine sank below the mountains. She re-emerged holding a large pair of metal shears. She walked over to Muriphany and put the shears to her neck. Charlie watched with horror as the sharp blades pressed against the helpless girl's flesh. "Stand back! This may spark," she warned. Wenzel and Charlie immediately stepped back and shielded their eyes. Professor Longtree counted to three to steady her shaking hands and then with all her strength closed the shears around the chain on Muriphany's necklace. As the shears cut through the gold,

Professor Longtree let out a horrible scream! A bolt of electricity shot from the chain and through Professor Longtree throwing her across the greenhouse! Then there was complete silence.

At that exact same moment, the Wyse and Mr. Ignas came running in! They saw what had happened and ran to Olive. She was breathing but unconscious. They straightened her body and covered her with some burlap to keep her warm until she woke up. After making sure Professor Longtree was safe, all four men ran to Muriphany. The chain had been broken and was lying on the floor burnt and smoking. Muriphany's neck had not been scorched. Olive's procedures had worked protecting the girl! Within a few minutes, Muriphany began to stir. She began moving her arms and legs. Soon, her eyes were open, and she lay staring at the four men. She looked at them with confusion.

But before a word of explanation could be spoken, a bell broke the silence with four loud rings! Mr. Ignas looked at the Wyse with intense worry. "We are under attack!" he exclaimed. Without hesitation, the Wyse looked at Wenzel and Charlie.

"Is it safe? The book! Is it hidden?" the Wyse demanded.

"Yes! It's hidden. What's going on?" Charlie said.

"The Lonely Manor has been seized! It is not safe here for you! I suspected this would happen. That's why I brought you these." He lifted a backpack with a canteen and rolled-up sleeping bag. "There are enough supplies to ensure your survival. You've been trained well, and now it is time for you to go. Remember the task at hand! You must save the Hill! We are all doomed if you don't!" With that, the Wyse handed Charlie and Wenzel their gear. He then picked up a third pack and handed it to Muriphany who had sat up on the table when the bells rang. "You must go with them, too. They need you as well!" Muriphany didn't know what to think, but her confusion was interrupted by four more loud rings of the warning bell! There was no time! Mr. Ignas ran to the back of the greenhouse, slid a large potted tree off a trap door, and signaled the three to enter. He handed each a lantern and wished them luck. When all three were down the ladder, he placed the tree back over the door and began to hide the evidence that they were ever there. He knew that soon the intruders would find the greenhouse. It was only a matter of time! The best thing they could do was make it hard to find the three people who were destined to save the Hill!

XX

20 Seized

In less than an hour, the intruders indeed had made their way to the greenhouse. Mr. Ignas slid Professor Longtree's body under a table full of hanging vines that created a wall to hide her unconscious body. Mr. Ignas then hid under a pile of old burlap seed sacks. It was just in time, too! He lay there holding his breath as he heard shoes clicking on the stone floor. The Wyse had escaped via a hidden passage in the wall to go to his office to secure some secret documents.

The footsteps slowed down as soon as they entered the greenhouse and cautiously walked around as if waiting for an ambush. When none came, the footsteps returned to normal and mumbled voices began speaking. Mr. Ignas could tell that the two intruders were males. Yet, they barely sounded human. Then he heard the footsteps head to the door, leaving the greenhouse! But instead of continuing on, the footsteps abruptly stopped! *What did I forget to hide?* Mr. Ignas thought to himself. Then he felt all the blood rush out of his face as he remembered. *Muriphany's necklace!*

The intruders knelt down and picked up the necklace off the floor. They held the charred piece of jewelry and examined it carefully. Suddenly, from directly across the room of the intruders, Professor Longtree began to stir! She was waking up at the worst possible moment! There was no way for Mr. Ignas to warn her without giving himself away. Before he could think of a distraction, the two intruders drew their swords and pulled Olive viciously from under the table by her foot! They pointed their swords at her neck as they waited for her to fight. Olive was so surprised she passed out again. Putting their swords away, the intruders carried Professor Longtree off!

Mr. Ignas sat paralyzed with fear. He kept going back and forth in his mind whether to fight to protect her or let them take her. She had no idea where Muriphany, Charlie, and Wenzel were. She didn't even know the Wyse sent Muriphany with Charlie and Wenzel. Mr. Ignas was surprised by that as well. The Wyse knew way more than he was leading on. Next time there was a chance, Mr. Ignas was going to question him about it. In the meantime, he had to somehow get the message of Professor Longtree's abduction to the Wyse!

Once the footsteps had clearly faded away, Mr. Ignas uncovered himself and cautiously made his way towards the secret door. In complete darkness, he used his hands to guide himself to the Wyse's personal office. Right when he thought he was there, he ran into a man! It was the Wyse! "Shh, don't make a sound," he whispered. The two men stood in complete silence, and that's when Mr. Ignas heard it. There were several other men tearing apart the office. They were clearly looking for something! Bang! A book hit the wall. Bang! Bang! Bang! Someone was throwing books across the room! Next, they heard the desk crashing to the ground as another intruder overturned it. They heard curtains ripping and glass breaking. Then they heard a low grunting voice shout something incoherent from another room. Immediately the intruders dropped what they were doing and left the Wyse's office.

"Did you make it in time?" Mr. Ignas asked.

"Yes, just barely," the Wyse replied breathing heavily.

Unsure how to tell him, Mr. Ignas nervously says, "They took Olive."

"How?" the Wyse asked angrily.

"I thought I got rid of all the evidence and hid Olive well, but when the intruders came in, I realized I left Muriphany's necklace on the floor! It was such a stupid mistake. The intruders must have stopped to pick it up because I heard them pause before they began to mumble to each other. That's when Olive began to wake up. I was completely covered so I couldn't see anything. My guess is that there were only two of them. Olive didn't say a word. She must have passed out after waking up to them standing over her. I let them take her. I figured she didn't know anything about where Charlie and Wenzel went, and she sure didn't know anything about

Muriphany going with them. Speaking of that, when did you decide to trust her?" Mr. Ignas asked.

Avoiding the question, the Wyse replied, "There's no telling where they will take her. She is a strong and witty woman, but we can only speculate who these intruders are and what they are after! She is in grave danger! We must assess the damage and find Olive!" At that, the Wyse burst through the hidden doors and entered his study. He quickly examined the room, then took off running down the secret passageway nearly knocking Mr. Ignas over. The tunnel was pitch black, but the Wyse had memorized the turns of the tunnel and was able to swiftly run through, turning at precisely the right time. It only took him a few minutes to reach the library. When he arrived, he pressed his ear against the hidden door and listened for any possible invaders. He heard nothing. Very cautiously he entered the library and made his way to the locked up scrolls. He didn't know what was being searched for but at least he could preserve what he knew was valuable information.

No sooner did the Wyse grab all the secret scrolls and enter the hidden passageway again, when more infiltrators burst through the library doors! The Wyse only made it within seconds. He stood on the other side of the hidden door with his heart pounding out of his chest. Once he caught his breath, he stood erect and listened to the trespassers. At first, the Wyse couldn't understand what they were saying. Their voices were mumbled and inhuman, but after a few minutes the Wyse recognized a word. They kept saying it as if they were talking about a person. The Wyse could not believe what he had heard! Then he heard it again! They were talking about Malek!

Adrenaline began to pump through the Wyse's body as he took in what he was listening to. He couldn't believe that Malek had infiltrated the Lonely Manor! It had never been done before! Knowing that Olive's life was in danger, and that Wenzel, Charlie, and Muriphany were on the run, the Wyse hid the scrolls in a secret compartment in the wall and burst through the door surprising the invaders dead in their tracks. He encountered three manlike creatures armed with clubs and daggers. Their bodies were slightly hunched, their heads were disfigured, and their skin looked like aged leather. They were caught completely off guard! The Wyse knew his advantage and within minutes disarmed them all. Using the cords from the library curtains, he tied up all three unconscious trespassers and dragged them into the secret tunnel. Within seconds of shutting the hidden door of the passageway, more invaders entered the library. Their voices were confused. They looked around for a few minutes, then took off running in another direction.

Mr. Ignas, having heard the commotion, came running to assist. Holding a poorly lit lantern, he saw the three unconscious intruders at the Wyse's feet. He quickly realized the situation had gone from serious to dangerous! Without talking, Mr. Ignas helped drag the infiltrators to the Manor's dungeon. It had been at least a hundred years since the dungeon was last used. Cobwebs heavily decorated the ceilings and walls like carefully hung garland. It was damp with a constant drip of musty water, and a strong smell of mold permeated the room. A few old lanterns hung timelessly on the walls. Some even still had a bit of oil in them. The Wyse lit a couple of the lanterns. He grabbed the cell keys off a rusted hook on the wall and opened the door nearest to where they were standing. Without talking, Mr. Ignas and the Wyse placed the tied intruders in the cell, locked it, and then left. Until they woke up, there was nothing they could get out of them.

From the dungeon, the Wyse was able to send out an alarm to the rest of the manor. The old dungeon alarm system was dusty and full of cobwebs, but its ring could still be heard throughout the whole Manor! Guards all around the estate now knew Malek was behind the invasion, and it was time to fight without restraint!

XXI

The Tunnel Escape

With only the light from their three small lanterns, the stairs seemed never-ending. Ever since they entered the tunnel, they had been walking down stairs. Sometimes the stairs took a sharp turn to the left or a gradual turn to the right. For about ten minutes the stairs swirled tightly downward. Charlie got so dizzy that he needed to stop and sit down.

For what seemed like hours, Wenzel, Charlie, and their new companion Muriphany, descended the tunnel stairs, legs shaking from fatigue. The walls were made of compacted dirt, which changed to hard red clay, and finally to cold damp rock. The lower they went, the damper and cooler it got. With Wenzel in front, the trio descended deep into the earth, far away from the unknown chaos above them.

Unsure of what to say to one another, especially to Muriphany, they walked mostly in silence. Their hearts were still pumping with adrenaline from the previous events. Now they were off to do what they had been trained to do, save the Hill!

"Wait a minute!" Wenzel exclaimed as he paused on the steps breaking the deafening silence.

"Do you hear that?" Charlie asked.

"It sounds like a river!" Muriphany exclaimed.

"Stay right behind me, and walk slowly. We don't know where the water starts. It'd be no good getting swept away. Mind your steps," Wenzel cautioned.

The trio slowly progressed forward, being extra cautious around turns, till finally, they reached the end of the stairs. Wenzel held his lantern high as he looked around the last corner. He took a long pause to listen. He could hear what sounded like an underground river, but he still couldn't see anything. Charlie and Muriphany were intently listening too. Slowly they walked around a corner and down what appeared to be another tunnel. At about thirty feet ahead of them, they began to see what they had been hearing. It was, in fact, an underground river!

"Shine your lights over there," Wenzel commanded. All three pointed their lights in the direction Wenzel told them to, and sure enough they saw it. A boat! It wasn't very big, just large enough to fit three to four people. Wenzel examined it closely to make sure it was safe to ride. It was!

The boat was tied to a stalagmite growing from the cave floor. By the looks of the rope and the rock growing over it, the trio concluded that the boat had been tied up for hundreds of years.

Incredible! It was as if it had been waiting for them all this time. As they were carefully getting into the boat, Charlie noticed something overhead. "Look at that, guys!" he shouted making, his echo travel down the river tunnel. Startled by the loud exclamation, Wenzel and Muriphany covered their heads anticipating trouble before looking at what Charlie was pointing at.

"There are lanterns hanging from the ceiling down the river!" Charlie pointed out with excitement.

"And this!" Muriphany said, picking up a long stick with one end wrapped in linen.

"The linen is soaked in oil, too!" Wenzel said as he grabbed the stick to examine it closely. "We can use it to light the lanterns as we float by!" Excitement began to fill them all.

Things were falling into place perfectly. Whoever made this tunnel must have been thinking a lot about escaping unnoticed by the above world. It was incredible! Who knew what surprises they would find next!

Reaching into his bag, Wenzel pulled out a set of matches. With a quick swipe, their torch was aflame. He touched the torch to the first lantern, and to their surprise a stream of fire connected each lantern to the other. Within minutes, the tunnel was lit as far as they could see. They turned off their handheld lanterns to save the oil for a future need. Quickly, they hopped in the boat excited to see where it would take them. Then, Muriphany took a dagger from her bag and effortlessly cut the rope free.

The current of the river was strong, and it easily carried the small boat down the tunnel. Occasionally, the three needed to use an oar to push the boat away from the wall, but for the most part, the river did all the work. Not knowing how long they would be traveling, the three took turns sleeping. After losing track of time, the three found themselves awkwardly sitting in silence.

"I wonder what food is in our backpacks," Charlie said breaking the silence. He grabbed his bag and began to rummage through it, until he found a sack of biscuits and a canteen. The others followed suit as if they just remembered they were hungry too. The three once again found themselves sitting in silence eating their slightly sweetened biscuits.

"Must be made with Professor Longtree's honey," Wenzel concluded while examining the biscuit he had just bitten into and wanting to break the silence.

"Yes, they're pretty good," Charlie added. Muriphany said nothing. Instead she just looked down and ate her food.

"So, where are you from Muriphany?" Wenzel inquired. Muriphany suddenly stopped chewing and stared up at Wenzel in surprise.

"Um, I don't know why you want to know about that. It's not like we are heading that way anyway," she said trying to end the conversation. Though her answer was a bit rude, there was a tenderness and a gentleness just below the surface that seemed to be fighting to get out.

"Do you have any family, then? Or have you been alone forever?" Wenzel shot back in irritation. He was surprised to see tears well up in her eyes as she fought to keep her composure.

Looking down at her lap, she said, "My mother died when I was born, and my father has always been distant. So, yes, I have always been quite alone."

Feeling guilty for his insensitive question, Wenzel replied, "I'm sorry. I didn't mean it like that."

"It's strange, isn't it?" Charlie piped in, but after seeing Wenzel's obvious glare, Charlie decided he should elaborate a bit. "I mean, the three of us, sitting in a lantern lit tunnel, eating honey biscuits, and waiting for our purpose on the other end of this tunnel! Who would have ever thought three people so different were the ones chosen to save the Hill!" At the mention of the Hill, Muriphany blushed, but it went unnoticed by the other two.

"I guess it is all very incredible," Wenzel admitted, "I just hope we make it in time. Who knows what danger is awaiting us. The Manor could be completely seized by now. My hope is we can find allies before it's too late."

"We will," Muriphany jumped in, "We have to!"

After a seemingly endless boat ride, suddenly a light appeared at the end of the tunnel. The river had been gradually declining, and within minutes, the boat came out with a splash on the side of a mountain into a glassy lake shadowed by other snowcapped mountains. The sun was shining bright and the warmth of the air was refreshing after being in a damp, cool tunnel.

Charlie and Wenzel rowed to shore and tied the boat up to a tall, skinny rock. Primarily focusing on getting their packs onto dry land, they failed to notice Muriphony's sudden agony. Arching her body and holding her back in excruciating pain, she was unable to get out of the boat on her own. Wenzel noticed first and ran to her side. "Muriphany, what is wrong?!" Wenzel demanded with concern. Unable to speak, and shocked by the pain, she continued to squirm in agony.

"Get her out of the boat and lay her on the sand," Charlie urged already beginning to pick her up. The two young men lifted her out causing her to scream even louder. Not sure what to do, Charlie and Wenzel laid her on the sand carefully, and watched her suffer alone. They had no idea what was going on or what they should be doing.

"The st-stones!" Muriphany moaned and pointed to another tall, skinny rock further from shore on a grass hill. Charlie looked to where she was pointing and saw seven glowing stones! Without thinking, he ran to the stones, grabbed them in his shirt, and brought them back to Muriphany. With a shriek of pain, she rolled over and pulled up her shirt, revealing a full back glowing dragon tattoo! Charlie's jaw dropped. He recognized that same tattoo from Skins' back!

Not knowing why Charlie was hesitating, Wenzel grabbed the stones from his hands and placed the seven smooth stones on the seven glowing spaces on Muriphany's back. As soon as the last stone was placed, Muriphany's agony ceased. Charlie and Wenzel sat silently wondering, who was this strange girl? *How did she now about the stones, and why did they perfectly fit into glowing places on her strange tattoo?* Wenzel thought.

Still staring at her, Charlie said, "I've seen those before! These are my skipping stones!" He pointed to the three rocks that had disappeared from Lake Thompson. "And these must be Uncle Ralph's," he said even more confused. Not wanting to give away his noticed connection between her tattoo and Skins' tattoo, Charlie chose to tell Wenzel about it later in private.

Before any of them could say another word, sounds like thunder were heard in the distant east. Muriphany sat up, letting the remaining stones fall to the ground. She acted as if she no longer needed them, and it was as if she knew what was happening next. They froze in place as they listened to the deafening sounds became louder. Charlie and Wenzel waited in fear. Muriphany waited with great anticipation. Then from above the snowcapped mountains they saw a cloud of large birds flying towards them. As the cloud of animals flew closer, the overwhelming sound became unbearable. The three covered their ears and looked away. *Connecting Muriphany's tattoo with the glowing stones must have summoned the large birds,* Charlie thought.

They really are coming to me! Muriphany internalized with hope.

When the forceful flapping ceased, the ground shook like an earthquake as the creatures landed. The trio uncovered their ears and looked toward the beasts, amazed at the sight! They weren't birds at all, but seven of the most beautiful dragons imaginable! Each dragon was colored differently in shiny scales. They stood about twenty feet tall with tails twice the length of their height.

Their wing spans were forty feet wide. *No wonder their flying was deafening!* Wenzel thought to himself, still awestruck. The claws on their feet were intimidating as they scratched at the beach, pulling huge piles of sand up without effort. Their sharp teeth peered out from their closed jaws. One could only imagine what damage they could do!

XXII

Moon Stones

The seven dragons kept to themselves as Charlie, Wenzel, and the recovering Muriphany explored the field on the hill. It was long and flat except for seven green mounds. They were spread out as if they were markers for something. Muriphany carried the sevens skipping stones carefully in a small leather pouch on her side. Charlie kept a close suspicious eye on her. He did not trust her. He feared she was a spy for Malek. But before Charlie had a chance to talk to Wenzel, Muriphany shouted, "Come look at this!" The two walked over to the mound where she was standing. "The moss on this mound wipes off and take a look at these markings," she said. Charlie was speechless. Under the moss was a large boulder. All the boulders were about the same height and width. The top of them revealed ancient markings and an impression the exact same size as one of the seven skipping stones, the stones that summoned the dragons. The trio looked at each other in amazement. Muriphany was filled with excitement while Charlie and Wenzel felt more unsure then ever.

"What could these be?" Wenzel asked out loud.

"Let's uncover the rest to find out!" Muriphany exclaimed bursting with delight. Charlie rolled his eyes. His suspicion made him cold towards anything Muriphany showed enthusiasm for. As she ran ahead to another mound, Charlie grabbed Wenzel's arm.

"I need to talk to you," he said. "It's about Muriphany and the tattoo. I've seen it . . . " But before he could finish, Muriphany ran up to them grabbing Wenzel and dragged him to a mound.

"See? It's the same. Let's put the stones on each one and see what happens!" she exclaimed showing more life than she had ever since they first met at the Manor.

"I don't know," Charlie interjected. "Last time we put the stones on something, these huge man-eating beasts came out. Just because they haven't eaten us yet doesn't mean they won't! I don't want any other crazy beasts showing up out of the earth or something, like man-eating worms!"

"Oh, relax, Charlie," Wenzel said. "I think we are onto something here. Besides, if these dragons are willing, then they will help us fight Malek." At the sound of his name, both Charlie and Muriphany shivered.

"There. All seven stones are on," Muriphany quickly added, stepping back to see what it would do. The three stood there frozen for several minutes waiting for something to happen, but nothing did. "That's strange. I thought . . . " Muriphany stopped herself from saying more.

"Thought what?" Charlie pushed suspiciously.

"I thought something would happen," she said.

"By the way, what's with the dragon on your back?" Wenzel pressed.

"And how did you know about the stones, and the mounds? And like everything else going on right now?" Charlie interrogated further. For what seemed like an eternity, Muriphany stood staring at the ground trying to figure out what to say.

"Well? There's a lot you aren't telling us. Who are you? Where did you come from?" Wenzel sternly asked. Muriphany broke out in tears and ran away towards the beach near the dragons.

Wenzel rolled his eyes as Charlie mumbled, "Good grief!"

That night they ate their dinner in silence. It seemed to be how things went lately. The dragons had caught more fish than they could eat so Charlie and Wenzel cooked some over a fire on the beach as the dragons napped around them. They were surprisingly docile creatures especially compared to their appearance.

As the sun finally sank its last rays of light below the glistening lake waves, the moon peered from behind a cloud, and a strange glow arose from the top of the mound-covered hill. Without a word, Muriphany instinctively jumped up and ran to the field where she earlier had placed the stones. Of course, Charlie and Wenzel chased after her, incredibly suspicious of her every move.

To their amazement, every boulder was glowing! Suddenly they heard loud flapping noises coming at them. Turning around, they saw the dragons were flying towards the mounds. Each one landed near a glowing boulder, placing a terrifying claw on top. Then in unison, the seven dragons bowed down to Muriphany, Charlie, and Wenzel. Muriphany's tattoo warmly glowed at their obedience to the trio.

XXIII

Olive's Imprisonment

Olive woke up strapped to a table with a terrible headache. The last thing she remembered was trying everything she could to save Muriphany's life, but now no one was in sight. She tried to sit up but to no avail. Her kidnappers had tied her securely down. She could hear commotion outside the door. Inside the room were a few chairs, a small window with the curtain drawn, and a bookshelf in the corner which was spilled all over the floor. Olive knew in her heart that something has gone terribly wrong. Mr. Ignas and the Wyse were nowhere in sight. The kids were missing as well, and the noises she heard outside the door weren't human. Suddenly she heard the ringing of the alarm bells! Her suspicions were confirmed, and she knew she had very little time to escape before Malek's men would torture her for information.

Observing she was tied down with old-looking rope, she began to look for weak points. She saw two sections where the rope was frayed thin, one spot near her right ankle, and one near her left knee. The kidnappers failed to search her pockets, and she could still feel the small herb spade inside her petticoat. With a little difficulty she reached the spade, but before she could pull it out, something heavy hit the floor. She had managed to accidentally knock a glass vase off the table. Olive froze and closed her eyes waiting for someone to check on her. When the door didn't open, she pulled out the spade and reached her strapped arm as far down as she could to the frayed rope near her knee.

Sawing back and forth for what seemed like hours, it was finally down to the last thread when the door came flying open. Her kidnappers burst in and were furious to find she had almost escaped. With inhuman-like sounds, the abdicators lurched forward pushing her down harder on the table. As one held her painfully in place, the other grabbed more rope and began to tie her tighter to the table. As they were doing this, Olive heard steady patient footsteps echoing down the hall. It was strange that in all that commotion, someone would be so calm. Barely able to breathe, Olive remained as still as possible with her eyes fixed on the doorway. The kidnappers heard the footsteps too and quickly stood up in attention to the door. They all waited with baited breath, Olive mostly because of the rope.

Suddenly the footsteps stopped right before the door. At first, Olive could not see who it was, then after what seemed like an eternity of waiting and her heartbeat echoing in her head, a man stepped through the door. It didn't take an introduction to figure out who it was—Olive's heart dropped as she stared at the face of Malek!

Malek was not very tall and quite slim with an undertone of muscle. Stature did not affect his authority, for the hate in his eyes brought the biggest giant to it's knees. The temperature of the room cooled, and the air became thin in his presence. Pure evil oozed out of every part of his being. Dressed in all black attire except for some red trim on his cloak, he slowly clicked his pointy black shoes in the direction of Olive. Olive's heart began to race. She was terrified!

Holding Muriphany's scorched necklace in his fist, he shouted in the most shrilled hate-filled voice, "Where is she?!" Olive closed her eyes in fear. Getting within inches of her face and placing both hands on her, he shouted again, "I said, where is she?!"

Afraid not to answer, Olive replied, "I don't understand why you would think I would know?"

Unsatisfied with her reply, Malek, with more hate in his eyes than before, flipped the table over with Olive still attached. "Do you really think I'm this stupid? Do you really think you can avoid telling me everything I want to know? This is MY Manor now! You belong to me!" he shouted maniacally. Olive, with tears running down her face began to hyperventilate. She was so scared and didn't know how to get out of this alive.

In fact, she did not get out alive. In a psychotic rage, Malek murdered the sweet Professor Longtree. Hatred burned inside Malek as he thought about her love and kindness until he could not contain his anger. Even the guards who imprisoned Olive were taken back and frightened for their own lives.

XXIV

The Cover of Darkness

As Charlie, Wenzel, and Muriphany stood admiring the scene before them, and somehow deep inside understanding the magnitude of that moment, they all felt a sudden deep urge to return to the Manor. It was as if the seven bowing dragons were speaking straight to their hearts. "Something is wrong at the Manor," Wenzel began, "I can feel it in my bones."

"But we don't know the way back," Charlie pointed out discouragingly.

"No, but they do," Muriphany said as she walked over to one of them. Charlie and Wenzel looked at each other in disbelief.

"You're not thinking of riding one of these things," Charlie questioned. "I can barely ride a horse!"

"It's true. I've seen him," Wenzel said comically. Charlie shot him a look. Wenzel stopped giggling.

"Yes, I do plan on that and don't worry. Look!" Muriphany motioned the boys to come over and look at the back of the dragon she was standing beside. To their amazement, built into their scales, or grown into their backs would be more like it, were perfectly shaped saddles of smooth dragon skin. The saddles dipped down lower than the other muscle as to provide a bit of shelter and security. There was even a perfect ridge to hold onto.

"Wow! I have never imagined anything like this before. Muriphany, we must go back to the Manor immediately! Something is gravely wrong, but when things calm down, you have some major questions to answer. And if things go wrong and you betray us, please be warned that we will not hesitate to act accordingly," Wenzel sternly warned.

Muriphany looked down at her feet and sheepishly kicked at the ground while trying her best to hold back the tears. "I understand. You can trust me. You will see," she said and then without hesitation climbed onto the dragon's back.

Charlie picked the orange hued dragon with a longer tail. Wenzel hesitatingly climbed onto the back of one with horns. To their surprise, the saddles were very comfortable and secure. Before the boys could exchange words, the dragons began their thunderous flapping. Within seconds, the trio, along with the seven dragons, were en route to the Manor. The creatures instinctively knew where to go. The Presence was much bigger than Charlie and Wenzel had originally thought, even the dragons seemed to hear its voice. They had no choice but to blindly trust that the Presence was indeed behind all this.

By cover of darkness they flew at speeds faster then any creature they had ever seen before. It was as if the wind was pushing them along, urging them to move faster. In fact, there was such an urgency in all of this that Wenzel, Charlie, and Muriphany almost could not enjoy the thrilling experience of soaring through the night sky. Above them in the moonless sky, millions of stars glowed like bright gems. The cool air raced across their backs, almost as if it was trying to blow away all their worries, and for a second it almost worked. But the urgency that ran through their bodies like fire could not be ignored!

Within a few hours, the Lonely Manor came into view. It was a horrible, stomach-wrenching sight. From out of nearly every window were tall flames! It had been entirely seized by the enemy! Panic ran through the trio as the seven dragons flew closer. They hadn't talked about a plan or even anticipated this level of disaster, but the dragons quickly calmed their spirits as they flew in formation confidently towards the burning building. They knew exactly what they were supposed to do, and the cover of darkness was giving them the exact advantage and element of surprise they needed.

Right before they reached the Manor, the seven dragons split formation and began surrounding the building. Before Malek and his followers were aware of the counterattack, the dragons began devouring anyone they saw. It didn't matter if it was one or twenty, the dragons took them down. Muriphany, Charlie, and Wenzel tucked low in their saddles for protection and stability, but the erratic movement of the dragons induced horrible motion-sickness. The trio, unknowingly to each other, were all throwing up as the dragons whipped around the Manor, spewing fire, and clawing down the enemies. The attack seemed like it took hours, but in reality it was less than thirty minutes before Malek and his goons were running for their lives into the mountains that surrounded the Manor.

Muriphany, catching her breath, and regaining her strength, sat up on her saddle and peered down at the fleeing enemies. She knew exactly where they were headed, and who was leading them. She wanted so badly to force her dragon to follow and take down Malek, but the dragon refused to listen to her longings. She had to let them go for now. They needed to find the Wyse, Mr. Ignas, and Professor Longtree, immediately!

The seven dragons, as if they had been there before, began one-by-one to land around the exterior walls of the Manor. The power of their wings created gusts of wind strong enough to snuff out almost all the fires inside. Thankfully, the stone exterior retained its former integrity. The fires were only superficial. As soon as the dragons landed, the trio clumsily dismounted. Charlie fell to the ground and laid there until the world stopped spinning around him. Unfortunately, his stomach was not finished displaying its disapproval of riding on an attacking dragon. Wenzel and Muriphany were only slightly more graceful but still suffered the same consequences.

Once the three of them had recovered a bit, they ran into the Manor without many words. As if they all were thinking the same thing, they ran through the scorched hallways in search of their friends. At every turn, they saw bodies of people they recognized. Some were badly injured, and some were gone. Tears ran down Charlie's cheeks as he charged forward making his way to the Wyse's office. Wenzel and Muriphany were right there with him, their faces stained with tears as well. Without saying a word, the trio pushed their way into the office. Their hearts dropped as they saw that it was completely destroyed. The fire had demolished almost everything. Everything except exposing the entrance to the secret tunnel in the walls. Wenzel pushed through the still smoldering debris and made his way to the wall of the tunnel. The three worked together to clear debris off from it, and just as they were about to open it, the secret door flung open and two men came barreling out plowing them down. Wenzel quickly grabbed the closest object to use as a weapon. It was a broken chair. Just as he was about to hit the two intruders, Charlie shouted, "STOP!" Wenzel froze just in time. It was the Wyse and Mr. Ignas!

For a minute, the five of them stood in silence waiting for their hearts to stop racing and their breathing to ease. "What are you doing here?" demanded the Wyse after he had caught his breath. "It's not safe. You are jeopardizing everything by being here!" he shouted in anger and shock.

"Hold on a second," Mr. Ignas chimed in. "Did you guys have anything to do with the dragons that just attacked the Manor?" he asked with a slight smirk.

"Um, yes," Charlie answered sheepishly.

"Can I see them!?" Mr. Ignas asked nearly jumping out of his skin.

"You can't," Muriphany gloomily stated, "They just left." She was standing by the window watching the seven magnificent beasts take flight heading to who knows where.

The rest of them rushed to the window and watched partly in awe and partly depressed. "Why'd they leave us?" Charlie asked.

"Perhaps further questions about the dragons should wait. We are grateful for their service to the Manor, but right now we have to secure the premises and attend to the wounded. And we need to find Olive. She was taken!" the Wyse said with anguish in his voice.

"Sir, the three of us will search high and low until we find her!" Wenzel promised and then led the way out of the office.

It was a depressingly long search through devastation. Injured and deceased lay helplessly in the hallways as others ran to help them. Smoke continued to fill the rooms and halls. Books, furniture, and old relics smoldered slowly for hours. Guards of the Manor worked relentlessly to prevent the fires from starting again. Prisoners were dragged away to the dungeon, and a surreal feeling took over the Manor. It was no longer an impenetrable fortress. Now it lay savagely attacked and vulnerable. Wenzel, Charlie, and Muriphany ran room-to-room shouting and eagerly searching for Professor Longtree. The time seemed to pass in slow motion. Each room they searched unsuccessfully left a pit of dread in their stomachs. Would they ever find her?

XXV

When All Seemed Lost

It was a quiet moonless night. Even the crickets seemed to mourn the loss of Professor Longtree with their silence. She was gone, taken away unfairly by evil. No one could sleep that night. Charlie, Wenzel, and Muriphany had indeed found her. Still tied to the table, her body was buried under debris. She had managed to scratch the word Malek into the wood with the point of her signet ring. The Wyse held that ring now, lovingly caressing it between his fingers. Even in her dying moment, she thought of helping them. They had buried her in what was left of her beloved garden. The Wyse, Mr. Ignas, Charlie, Wenzel, and Muriphany lit a fire to keep warm. No one wanted to leave. They all sat contemplating the last few days' events. So much had changed. So much had been lost. The fire crackled softly, barely breaking the silence. Suddenly, Charlie jumped up, and ran like mad towards the Manor!

"Charlie! Where are you going?" Wenzel shouted after him while standing to his feet feeling confused and concerned.

Without much time and with a burst of adrenaline Charlie only replied, "THE BOOK!" Everyone had forgotten about the book. There had been so much distraction and turmoil, that the book had slipped their minds. In an instant, they all raced after Charlie. They felt the same urgency to secure its safety.

When they reached the Manor, they found Charlie savagely throwing debris right and left inside what used to be his room. The others just stood there watching, not knowing how to help. With one final grunt and throw, Charlie managed to clear a small space revealing the wooden floor. He grabbed a piece of broken metal and pried up a floor board. Everyone held their breath waiting to see the book. Charlie frantically patted down the dark hole. "NO!" he shouted in a panic. Immediately, Wenzel jumped down on his knees, pushed Charlie out of the way and stuck his whole arm in. In a what seemed like time standing still, they all waited. Finally, Wenzel pulled out his arm, and to everyone's relief, he was grasping a very soot-covered book.

Charlie began to weep from the emotion of it all. He had just lost Professor Longtree. He could not bear losing the book to the enemy, too. Wenzel placed an understanding hand on his shoulder and leaned against the debris in exhaustion. The Wyse gently grabbed the book from Wenzel's hand and opened it.

It read:

For months, the townspeople have been living within the protection of the Secret Keepers. They have been gaining strength, not only mentally, but numerically, too.

Allies from all over the land have been showing up along similar clay paths. They, too, have felt the threat of attack from Malek. They feel an unwavering unity to stop Malek from destroying the world as they know it. Now, with each day, the townspeople and allies train side-by-side. Boys are becoming soldiers, women and children are becoming skilled craftsmen and blacksmiths, and the elderly cook and clean. Everyone puts in their all. The last key to the victory of the battle is for Wenzel, Charlie, and Muriphany to join the ranks with their unique skills and giftings. So hurry up, Wenzel, Charlie, and Muriphany, you are needed!

The Wyse looked up from the book with his mouth still open. The book was speaking to them at that very moment! "Well, best be getting you three on your way again," chimed in Mr. Ignas with that same smirk from earlier.

"In the locked scroll volt, I have an ancient map with directions to approximately where the Secret Keepers are located. You will take that with you, and leave immediately," the Wyse instructed.

Without any more time to rest or recover, the trio found themselves in a frenzy trying to repack their backpacks. Unsure of the voyage ahead, it was hard to decide what to take. "Shouldn't we take the book?" Charlie asked the Wyse.

"No, I am afraid that is much too dangerous. I have locked it in the scroll volt. You will take this instead," the Wyse said, unrolling the scroll with the ancient map.

The five of them stood staring and studying the map. Suddenly, Mr. Ignas turned white as the blood drained from his face! With a shaky finger, he pointed to a section of the map labeled, "The Land of the Giants." "Beware," he said with a hoarse voice, "For the land you will cross, the one with giants, does not fare well on travelers. Very few who have traveled there have ever continued their journey."

Before anyone could reply, a huge gust of wind burst open the window panes, strongly swirling around the room. When it settled down, there was a clear arrow made from the debris on the floor. "Your journey has begun," The Wyse said, "It is time for you to leave."

So, Wenzel, Charlie, and Muriphany quickly threw on their backpacks, rolled up the scroll, and ran out in the direction of the arrow.

XXVI

The Land of Giants

By lunch time they had already been walking for many hours. Since they took off while it was still night, it was a surprise to them they still had enough energy to continue. "We should stop here and rest a bit," Wenzel suggested. He had naturally assumed the role of team leader. The others weren't opposed to it at all. In fact, at times Charlie was relieved to not have to make the decisions. They threw down their packs against a tall oak tree and leaned against its trunk. A clear creek flowed alongside them, and they drank refreshingly to their satisfaction. After a few minutes of sitting, they began to feel tired and all three fell asleep.

The next morning they woke up completely surprised by how much they had slept. The sun was just starting to rise as they put their packs on when a strong wind blew and revealed a path for them to take. Wenzel checked the map and saw something that made his heart jump. He hesitantly informed the others. Fear bellowed up inside them. They knew they had to soon cross the Land of the Giants! Mr. Ignas's warning echoed through Wenzel's head, "Beware. For the land you will cross, the one with giants, does not fare well on travelers. Very few who have traveled there have ever continued their journey."

"Giants!" Wenzel said. "We can't escape from man-eating giants! There has to be another way." Knowing the importance of the success of this quest, the three headed off to their fate. They knew before the day was over they'd be face-to-face with giants!

Time went by slowly. It seemed like the more they thought about the giants the heavier each step became. Secretly, each hoped they made a wrong turn as they pushed their way through the thick brush, when suddenly they came in direct confrontation with the giants! They were huge giants alright, but they weren't the kind they'd been expecting. They were giant plants! The trees were average size, but dandelions, blades of grass, and mushrooms were all eye level or taller. What an amazing feeling to be shaded by foliage that ordinarily only comes up to your ankle!

"What danger is there here?" Muriphany said to the others.

"No danger at all," a voice from nowhere said, "nothing really ever goes on here."

They all looked high and low searching for the source of the voice. Then Wenzel caught a glimpse of a man lying in a hammock between two giant daisies. He had a familiar face and wore a straw hat over his eyes. "Sorry," Wenzel said, "I didn't see you there." Not knowing what else to do, they walked up to the man and recognized him instantly as Mr. Ignas!

"What are you doing here, Mr. Ignas?" Charlie blurted rudely, "I thought you told us to be careful in the Land of the Giants?"

The man sat up slightly and tipped his hat up to see the three standing in front of them. "Mr. who?" He said. "Lads and lass, I don't know what you're talking about. Mr. Ignas . . . huh," the man said trailing off. Before the man lay back down in his hammock, he paused as if remembering something. But, as if the memory was too much effort to recall, he fell back asleep.

The three continued past the strange man. Not sure what to think about him, they decided it was best to let him sleep and get through the land of the giants as quickly as possible. As they walked, they saw all sorts of odd things hanging in the giant vegetation. Pocket books, hats, jewelry, packs, cloaks, pillows, and pictures were all carefully placed in the foliage. It was as if people found these things and then placed them in the giant plants for the owners to find, but the further they walked, the more stuff they saw hanging. No one seemed to claim back their objects. As they walked, they began to feel sleepy again even though they had just rested. With each step deeper into the Land of the Giants, they yawned and longed to lie down. Starting to take off their packs to rest, suddenly out of nowhere, the sleepy stranger tackled Wenzel, stopping him.

"NO!!!!" the man shouted. "Run!!!!! Run! And don't stop until we are out!" With renewed energy, the four took off running as fast as they could. Their hearts pounded out of their chests, and all their senses were on high alert. After what seemed like an eternity, the edge of the Land of the Giants was in sight. They could run just a few more minutes and be out. When Charlie looked back to see if Muriphany was able to keep up, he watched as she tripped and fell flat on her face! Instantly, he stopped and turned around to help her. When he reached her, he sat down next to her and began to sleep. The stranger and Wenzel arrived at the end of the Land of Giants, but to their horror saw the other two sleeping in the path. The stranger slumped over with his hands on his knees to catch his breath, then without consulting Wenzel, darted back in to retrieve Charlie and Muriphany. Knowing that one person couldn't do it alone, Wenzel dashed in after. Unable to awaken Charlie or Muriphany, the stranger and Wenzel dragged them out. Once safely out of harm's way, in pure exhaustion, Wenzel and the stranger dropped the sleeping friends and passed out next to them.

A few hours later all four of them began to wake. The sun was lowering now, and the cool of the night was settling in. Without much talking, they managed to make a fire as they thought about what had just happened. Once they were comfortable by the fire, the stranger spoke up. "I couldn't stop thinking about what you said. I even dreamed about this Mr. Ignas. I realized just in time that I indeed knew who he was. I am he. Except, I am not the Mr. Ignas you probably referred to. That Mr. Ignas is my twin brother! We came here together years ago. I had completely forgotten until you said his name, our name." Charlie, Wenzel, and Muriphany just stared at him in disbelief.

"Years ago when we were young and full of adventure, we said good-bye to our mother and took off on a quest to learn about the world. We had grown up hearing stories and legends that never left our imaginations. We had to see them, experience them, and learn from them. Sadly, when we came here, I ignored the warning signs. I was much less cautious than my twin brother. I allowed the giants to hypnotize me. I embraced the laziness of the land and slowly forgot everything. I am not the only one in that place. There are others just like me who sleep the days away, and when we are awake we find things and place them in the plants for the owners to retrieve. Now that my mind is clear, I know that those very things belonged to us. We all just went mad and forgot we owned them. Seems pretty ridiculous now," the second Mr. Ignas said trailing off a bit. Then looking up at them suspiciously, he asked, "What are two young lads and a lass like you doing in these parts anyway? What kind of mischief are you up to? And where is my brother?"

Almost at once, the three began explaining to the second Mr. Ignas the whole situation. It was a messy explanation filled with interrupting each other and talking over one another. The second Mr. Ignas held up his hand and said, "Hold on a minute. You three are acting as if your brains are still fogged. I think I've got the gist of it. If what you say is true, then we have no time to waste. I must take you to Traitors' Island. The Traitors will want to meet you!"

XXVII

Traitors' Island

They had reached Traitors' Island much easier than they had expected. Mr. Ignas's twin brother, Mr. Ignas, whom they now called Ren, said that long ago he had heard a secret tale about 17 traitors of Malek trapped on an island. After studying maps and land proximity, he and his twin brother, Mr. Ignas, had guessed where the island might have been. Ren said that his brother would be proud to know that indeed they were right!

Now they found themselves standing face-to-face with the 17 traitors who had quite a story to tell. In fact, the traitors were not surprised by their arrival at all. They said the Presence had shown them four allies would make their way to the island to rescue them. Around a fire listening intently, Charlie, Wenzel, Ren, and Muriphany listened to the group tell their incredible tale.

A man by the name of William spoke with sincerity and authority. He said, "Fall was upon us and so was the annual Shrinking Pond ritual for those coming of age. You see, anyone who wanted to be an adult in the Land of Arar had to enter into the Shrinking Pond. It was said that if you chose not to go into the water at the appointed time, you would be banished, sacrificed to the Beast, or killed on the spot, depending on Malek's mood. As you can imagine, no one chose not to, until us. At first, we all thought the pond's name was insignificant, but the more we thought about it, the more we saw there was evil magic in the pond. Malek used it to control the minds of his people, the only true power he still has.

Once you've entered the water of the Shrinking Pond, any hopes of a better life are dissolved immediately. It left you feeling like it was all a distant dream swept far away by the wind. By law, it is required for everyone to bathe in the pond on their 18th year and every five years thereafter. It is disguised as a celebration of the coming of age, and it sadly has become a cherished ritual. Huge feasts are thrown, games are played, and for a short moment, there is a false sense of joy in Arar. It truly is the only time we ever celebrated anything. We longed for something to celebrate.

But one night, when some of us were coming home from exploring the outer woods, we discovered a dark magic that controlled the people. We came across an altar of some sort. At first we thought it was just some fallen boulders from a nearby mountain, but as we looked closer, we saw that it was detailed and man-made. Hidden under the mysterious altar was an ancient journal with a strange clock on it. And when the book was opened, Malek was revealed to us. We sat there all night reading it by the moonlight. We learned many horrid things about Malek that night. And during this time we had our first encounter with the Presence of the Hill. He came to us and spoke with us. For the first time in our post-Shrinking Pond lives, we had hope again and dreams for a better future. From then on, we knew something had to be done. We had to fight back! For months, we secretly met underground. We found caves and crevices in the earth where no living thing would dare go into but us. We planned and committed as a group not to turn back, no matter what happened! We knew we risked death, but Malek had to be challenged!

So over 19 years ago, we refused to bathe on our 5th anniversary. To our surprise, Malek didn't kill us. Instead, he sent us to a barren island to die of starvation and cold. What Malek didn't know was hidden behind mountains on the other side of the island, was a warm tropical current that flowed past the island creating a refreshing paradise. We are now sitting on that very spot.

We expected to die just as Malek intended, but the Presence of the Hill showed favor on us and guided us here. Not sure what was going on at first, we thought we were all hallucinating from the elements. We thought we were walking further into the barren wasteland to die, but the Presence was guiding us here day-by-day. It felt good to listen, and since we were so desperate, we figured there wasn't anything to lose. I am glad we did."

Muriphany took the first opportunity she had and slipped away from the campfire. The 17 traitors had been sitting around the fire telling Ren, Wenzel, and Charlie all the horrible and evil things Malek had done to them. Muriphany felt an overwhelming sense of guilt. It was as if the traitors were talking about her. It was obvious no one recognized her, yet the feeling of wrongdoing was unbearable! Her heart was pierced with pain as she heard the stories of torture that had been going on for generations after generations. She had to get away! The blood that caused the years of monstrosity in the Land of Arar was running through her veins. Malek was her father! When Muriphany could no longer stand hearing their stories, she took off running towards the peninsula that she had seen as they sailed to the island earlier. She thought that if she could just get there, then maybe she could escape the island!

When Wenzel, Charlie, and Muriphany were still within the walls of the Lonely Manor, Muriphany hid a terrible secret. The pendant she wore around her neck was a gift from her father and a curse. It was full of dark magic. Without warning, Malek would summon her. He sent her to the Lonely Manor disguised as *Skins* to spy on Charlie and Wenzel! His intention was for her to transform back into Muriphany, gather information from the Manor so that he could attack their weak spots, and use the dragons to destroy the Hill and its allies. But since Muriphany was not fully her father's blood, she did not have the same hate inside her heart. Therefore, the Presence of the Hill allowed her into the Lonely Manor. She has been running from her father ever since the night Charlie and Wenzel saw her faint in the hallway, the night she refused to follow her father.

Dashing through densely-forested trails proved difficult with only peeks of moonlight beaming through the foliage. Normally, Muriphany would have been spooked by the eery glow, but her determination to conceal her identity overrode her fear. She reached the end of the forest rapidly and began running down the peninsula as fast as she could move her tired feet. Not sure what she was going to do once she got to the end, she only knew she needed to get there quickly.

It was a full moon that night, and the light of the moon reflected off the water in hues of blue and silver. The waves were surprisingly gentle and everything seemed calm and peaceful. Arriving at the end of the peninsula, she threw herself down on the ground and let out a painful cry. She hated who her father was! She hated the destiny he had made for her! She longed to be free . . . "But how?" She whimpered out loud in a choked voice.

As her words drifted across the water, soft heavy footsteps came up behind her. She froze in fear! *They have discovered me!* She thought. But when she gathered enough courage to turn around, she was surprised to see a most beautiful creature. Staring back at her was a sleek black velvety panther! As it walked towards her, the movement of its muscles under its shiny fur glistened in the moonlight. To her surprise, Muriphany was not scared. Ironically, the panther's presence made her feel safe.

The animal gently approached Muriphany with compassion, placing his head to hers. Then she heard a voice:

"Do not be afraid Muriphany. I have sent this panther to you as a sign of my power. This wild beast can tear its prey from limb to limb, but I have made it a gentle kitten. I am the Presence that is in the Hill and have heard your cry. I can help you. Your father destined you for destruction, but I also have plans for you. I have seen your heart and choose to make you a great protector of the

Hill. If you wish to accept this future, stand up, and I will guide you . . . to the Hill . . . to your home."

Immediately, Muriphany felt something new inside her! She had been searching for a free life, a future all her own, and this was it! She stood up with confidence, as a new person no longer stained by the blood of her father. She faced out towards the sea waiting, but waiting for what? Seeing something move in the distant waters, she squinted and leaned forward. *Could it be?* she thought. Muriphany had heard stories of the mystical elephants. And now, here they were swimming to the island to rescue her!

XXVIII

Reunited

The stories of the 17 traitors were nothing short of miraculous. As Charlie, Wenzel, and Ren sat by the fire listening and discussing the fate of the Hill with the Traitors, Charlie felt a strange sensation behind him. He ignored it at first, thinking it was just his imagination gone wild. But then it happened again! Something tickled him behind his ear. This time it was followed by a deep purr. Charlie sat frozen in fear. Was he hallucinating? Was he just exhausted from this whole experience and was losing his mind? Then it stopped and everything was still.

Charlie let out a sigh of relief. It surprised him how tense he felt and how easily worked up he apparently was. Suddenly, it happened again! This time Charlie jumped out of his seat while slapping his ear in hopes to shoo away whatever was tickling his ear. The rest of the group grew silent as they stared at Charlie slapping himself. Wenzel almost began to laugh thinking that his friend had gone crazy, but before he could, from the darkness behind Charlie's seat, the purring could now be heard by the whole group. And as if time slowed down, a black panther, one pace at a time, emerged from the darkness.

The stealthy animal entered the group as if he owned the island. Its presence commanded the attention of everyone as it made its rounds, with muscles under glistening black fur revealing beastly power, a threat to the whole group. Its eyes glared around making contact with everyone. Then a voice spoke from within the panther as if they were hearing the panther's own thoughts. It was the Presence again, and it said, "Long have you been faithful. Long have you waited to stop Malek's madness," the Presence continued, "It is time to move. The elephants are waiting." At that, the panther ran off like a kitten chasing a mouse, and the herd of mystical elephants appeared. The huge creatures had come to take them off the island!

There was a bit of commotion as emotions ran high for the Traitors. They had been waiting and preparing for this moment for so many long years, but it had been such a long time that some felt paralyzed at first. Then William, a natural leader among the group, spoke up again saying, "Friends! All those years ago when we refused the Shrinking Ponds, when Trina and I left our baby boy in the Hill so that we could fight Malek, it was for this! Let's be brave! Let's fight and stop Malek once and for all!" As William's words rolled off his tongue, Wenzel's heart raced in his chest! The book he and Charlie had read was indeed about him and his parents!

As the rest of the group hurried about collecting their belongings and getting ready to leave the island on the elephants, Wenzel just stood there staring at Trina and William.

A thousand thoughts and feelings raced through his head. Then Trina's eyes locked with Wenzel's, and at that moment she knew who he was. She dropped the things that she had been gathering together and ran with all her might at Wenzel. She grabbed him and drew him in a deep embrace. Their hearts seemed to beat as one for the first time since he was born. Warm tears ran down their cheeks as they sank to the knees still embracing each other. William was just finished packing up their things when he noticed Wenzel and Trina on their knees sobbing. Immediately he knew. He ran to them and joined in on the joyous embrace. Forgetting about time and the task at hand, they just knelt there holding each other.

The trust that Trina and William had in the Presence of the Hill to give up their son to fight evil was proven true and real at that very moment. The Presence had returned Wenzel to them! Then suddenly they heard a voice, "It is time. The others have already left and are headed for the Secret Keepers, but I have a special plan for you. You will head up the South Mountains. The elephants can only take you so far, but I promise, just as I did before, I will protect you and provide a path for you." Without questioning the Presence, Wenzel and his parents stopped crying and looked around. Three elephants were left, loaded with supplies, and waiting for them. They each mounted an elephant immediately and began their journey to the South Mountains.

XXIX

Killing Grounds

Muriphany was exhausted. The emotional and physical strain she had been put through by her father had drastically taken its toll. The sway of the elephant as she sat atop it, soothingly put her to sleep. When she finally awoke, she had no idea how long she had slept or where the elephant had taken her. All she could tell was that they were on land now. But the land was nowhere she had ever been before. Yet, there was an unsettling familiarity to it. Muriphany swallowed hard as she sat up straight on the elephant to look around. The trees were dead and covered in a sickly black fungus. The smell of the air was similar to rotting flesh. The sun was dim behind yellowish clouds, and not one bird or animal could be heard, just the crunch of the elephant's feet on the dead leaves below. They were seemingly following a trail. After being on it for several more minutes, the elephant started to make a steady incline as if they were climbing a mountain. With each step up, Muriphany's heart ached and filled with dread. She could feel a heavy evil in these woods, and whatever was at the end of the trail, seemed far worse.

It took an hour for the elephant to reach a point in the trail where it leveled off onto a high plateau. Still in thick forest, Muriphany could not see a thing ahead, but the smell became much stronger. As they continued along the path, Muriphany began to hear groaning. At first she thought the noise was imagined but the sinking pit in her stomach told her it was much worse than that. Suddenly, the trail took a sharp turn to the left and then another to the right, until they finally emerged out of the thick trees and onto an open plain. Muriphany nearly fell off the elephant from the sight of horror in front of her. She knew her father had places like these, where he brought and tortured his enemies leaving them to die, but she had never herself seen one until now! Knowing her father wasn't currently there, she dismounted the elephant and stood staring out. She couldn't believe that the Presence had led her to her father's Killing Grounds. In her heart, she knew there must be a reason why she was brought here. The Presence wouldn't punish her or betray her. *There must be a purpose,* she thought!

Suddenly, from out of nowhere, a hand grabbed her ankle. She screamed as she turned around to see an injured, desperate man at her feet! She quickly dropped down to support the man's head as he tried to speak. "There are more of us here. We fought back," he struggled to say. "Please help us," he forced out before collapsing in her arms. With tears streaming down her dirt-stained face,

Muriphany continued embracing the man's head as she looked around to see where the others could possibly be.

Then she heard it, faint cries for help. She gently put the man's head down. Thankfully, he was still breathing. She jumped to her feet and started to run towards the sound. She ran just a few paces before the ground under her began to drop, she jumped back just in time as the earth gave way and exposed an underground cave. When the dust cleared, she saw them! There must have been thirty captives huddled, cold, and injured. Instantly, the tattoo on her back began to burn. She turned around quickly, terrified that maybe her father was returning to finish what he had started, but instead of seeing her father, she heard flapping. It grew louder and louder until she saw them again. The dragons were coming! Her heart burst with hope!

"Don't worry! I will get you out of here! You are safe now!" she shouted down to the prisoners.

Using the rope the dragons had brought, Muriphany was able to make a litter, a makeshift stretcher, to lift the injured prisoners from the cave. They were all hurt, cold, and hungry. A few of them had enough strength to walk. She helped them first onto the dragons' backs using rope to secure them. The dragons were patient and gentle as if understanding the situation and helping wherever they could.

It took a couple hours before all the injured people were either secured to the back of a dragon or laying on a makeshift litter to be lifted in the air by the beasts. Muriphany's heart ached for these people! A few of them told her what had happened. They said that as they were leaving the Hill, they were ambushed and about 100 of them were taken to the Killing Grounds. For weeks they sat in this cave. Malek would take some out to torture. Some would return to the cave, others did not. Malek did not give them food or water. If it hadn't been for a small cave stream and the insects that lived in the earth, they would have all died.

Tears again streamed down Muriphany's face as she mounted a dragon. Hugging its neck from behind she whispered, "Thank you." The dragon purred back to her as it lifted its wings and took flight. The rush of the air made Muriphany forget her despair for a moment, but as they reached the end of the South Mountains, horror struck her again. As she looked down, she could clearly see the devastation her father and his army had left behind. The earth was scorched and seemed to cry out in anguish. Smoke billowed from small villages and the few survivors could be seen running for cover from the dragons. Trusting that the dragons were taking her and the prisoners to safety, she continued looking down for any signs of trouble.

Unexpectedly, something whizzed past her head! She quickly turned, looking in the direction of where the object came from. And there on the ground was the largest army of her father's she had ever seen, and mounted on a mutilated beast in the very front, was her father holding the bow that shot the arrow at her! Her father was trying to kill her! But before she could react in any way, all the dragons double-backed, torching the earth in front of Malek. The smoke and chaos were enough of a distraction for them to get away before more shots could be fired. Muriphany's heart sank.

She knew her father would hate her for what she did, but for some reason, she didn't expect him to kill her. She was his own flesh and blood, but that didn't matter to him. Now, she was just an enemy, like the prisoners she had rescued from the cave.

Night was falling again, and the cover of darkness gave Muriphany enough comfort that she fell asleep from pure exhaustion. The dragons continued on without faltering. They were strong, beautiful creatures, so fierce yet so gentle. They flew for a few more hours until they reached the Secret Keepers, a hidden undisclosed oasis made from densely packed enchanted trees that no sound could penetrate. The Secret Keepers had been expecting the dragons. As soon as the dragons approached the magical forest, the trees moved to make a space for them to land safely inside. When the last dragon entered, the hole was instantly swallowed up by the thick impenetrable wall of leaves and branches.

XXX

On the Mountain

In just a few hours, the elephants reached the tree line of the tallest peak in the South Mountain Range. Trina, William, and Wenzel were weary from the long, cold journey. With each hour that passed and with every significant elevation gain, the temperature dropped and the wind increased. Finally, the elephants stopped and refused to go any further.

Wenzel dismounted the huge beast and then helped his mother down off hers. William jumped down from his elephant with ease and began untying their packs of supplies. It was clear it was time to continue on foot. After taking a short meal break, the newly united family lifted heavy packs onto their backs and said good-bye to the mystical elephants. But before they could take their first step onward, a new gust of wind swirled around them, pushing past. As they looked to the ground they saw that indeed another path had been revealed! The Presence wanted them to continue up beyond the tree line and head towards the glacier of the mountain.

As they bundled themselves up the best they could with the things they had, the thought of continuing forward gave them chills. Still, they trusted the Presence and trudged on. At first, the path was very steep with no other danger. Yet, the altitude made each step feel heavy and each breath of air left them wanting more. Soon the path became narrow with treacherous, steep cliffs on one side. Trina, William, and Wenzel hugged the mountain as they walked cautiously along the dangerous path. A few instances, they thought they'd never make it, but they continued on. Trina lost her footing at one point and nearly fell to her death if it had not been for the quick hand of her son Wenzel. Finally, after hours of climbing, they reached the snow peaks and dropped to the ground with exhaustion. Sick from elevation, they laid with their face against the cold snow.

In a strange way it felt refreshing to them. Extremely thirsty, Wenzel began to eat the snow. Suddenly a raspy voice warned, "You may be thirsty enough to drink a lake, but any more of that snow and you will die." All three of them were frozen and afraid to move. Unexpectedly, Wenzel felt a boney finger touch his back. He stopped breathing! "It's okay," said the voice, "I'm not here to hurt you, but before you turn around, I must warn you. My appearance is gruesome, and I may frighten you. Know this, Wenzel, I am a friend of the Presence of the Hill." Trina and William sat up in surprise and just stared in disbelief.

Initially, Wenzel was shocked and scared that this voice knew his name, but at the mention of the Presence, he felt a peace. With strong winds fiercely blowing around them, he gained enough courage to turn around. The sight was indeed horrific! Upon first glance, the creature looked to be in excruciating pain. His back was twisted causing one shoulder to be several inches lower than the other. His chest was sunken in and his crooked shoulders jutted forward. His left leg was shorter than his right causing an unnatural stance. In fact, nothing about him was natural. His face was deformed and a thick, dark scar covered his nose. The only "normal" feature was his eyes. "Let me help you up," it said, "I have much to tell!" Wenzel hesitatingly allowed the creature to help him up and lead him towards shelter. Motioning at Trina and William, he said, "First, I will feed you and get you warm."

His home was tucked away in a deep cave. It was simple but did not lack any of the comforts of the village homes on the Hill. The creature scurried around grabbing blankets, adding wood to the fire, and preparing hot cups of tea. Wenzel was amazed how fast the man-like being moved with its mangled body. "You must remove all your wet garments, or you'll freeze," it warned them.

Feeling too ill and tired to talk, Wenzel, Trina, and William didn't bother to protest. They simply did as they were told. Thinking rationally, it seemed taking off the wet clothes would make them colder. Though the thought of undressing was unbearable, their damp clothes clung frigidly to their bodies. To their surprise, they felt much warmer sitting by the fire wrapped in dry blankets. The creature hung the wet garments by the fire to dry. Having sat for several minutes warming, Wenzel felt strong enough to ask questions. Coming off unexpectedly rude, he blurted, "Who are you?" Realizing his tone, Wenzel softened his facial expressions to an apologetic glance.

"That's all right," it said, "I actually thought you wouldn't feel like talking until after you've slept. But now is as good a time as any," it paused before continuing, "I'm Kelam. I am the first-born of Malek. Not many know about me . . . " Noticing Wenzel's look of confusion and Trina and William's look of shock, he stopped talking. "Oh!" Kelam said with an epiphany, "I guess I have more explaining than I thought. She hasn't told you."

Even more confused, Wenzel blurted out, "Who hasn't told us what?" Seeing Wenzel's dismay, Kelam poured himself a cup of tea, then pulled a chair up to the fire.

"Let me finish explaining before you ask any further questions. Agreed?"

"Agreed," they all said.

"I'll begin, well . . . at my birth, I suppose. I was born 20 years ago by magic to Malek. The only purpose for my birth was to be trained to kill the chosen ones of the Hill. In other words . . . you and your friends." The creature paused and made eye contact with Wenzel. "You do know that you're one of the chosen ones?" Wenzel nodded affirmatively. "Good. But as you can see, I was born deformed and weak. Malek, in a fit of rage, scratched my face minutes after I was born. My mother and I were useless to him. She was killed, and I was thrown away. Why he didn't kill me, too, I do not know. Instead, I was left to die on my own. The Presence of the Hill rescued me from my fate. He brought me here to train and teach me. That is why I am here speaking to you. My strength is now above the average man. The Presence saw my life still had a purpose even though I was cursed. In my gratitude, I have chosen to stay loyal to the Hill and serve the Presence. Malek could never do it, that is why he seeks to destroy the Hill." Seeing that he was diverting he said, "I'll explain that tomorrow."

Wenzel was sitting at the edge of his seat with anticipation. Trina and William held hands closely together. Before the creature went on, he sipped his tea. Kelam continued, "Malek wasn't ready to give up on destroying you. You see Wenzel, Malek made a mistake when creating me. He did it by magic instead of by love. That is why I look the way I do. I was created with a hateful heart, a heart that sought revenge instead of love. Muriphany was made by love." Wenzel's eyes widened and his face turned pale. Trina and William shot glances at each other. They hadn't remembered seeing Muriphany on the island. "Things are beginning to make sense now," the creature noticed, "Her mother, whom Malek fell in love with after killing mine, died in childbirth, leaving Malek heart-broken once again. One thing Malek didn't realize was that the love Muriphany was created with, never left her. She hid it from her father as she grew up. She didn't want to disappoint him because she was an excellent fighter and deceiver, and love was a weakness in her father's eyes. Malek became very proud of Muriphany and was confident she'd kill you. What he didn't expect was for her to fall in love with you."

Wenzel's jaw dropped in surprise again! "I see you didn't know that either. Well, tonight, you'll have a lot to ponder over. Muriphany betrayed her father at the Lonely Manor the night you found her in the corridor. She was terrified you'd find out her true identity. That's why she ran from you. She's loyal to the Hill, and she has been in hiding with the others since her disappearance from Traitor's Island. The Presence has been mentoring her. She has yet to learn about me. She's not ready for that." Pausing again, the creature sipped the last of his tea. "I think that'll do for the night. You can sleep in the beds I've prepared for you. Oh yes, I knew you were coming," Kelam said with a grin, "Sleep on your thoughts, and I'll answer all your questions in the morning."

XXXI

Morning Death

The next evening, Malek came to the Killing Grounds to finish off the prisoners. As he approached the underground cave, he noticed that the earth was all disturbed with marks as if something had been dragged along it. Quickly, he ran to the cave and looked down in rage! With intense anger, he turned around, grabbing one of his loyal followers and threw him violently down into the cave.

After the initial scream from the fall, nothing else was heard. Malek, feeling his anger burn even more inside him, went into a full fury. Those around him who had come to help execute the prisoners stepped away in fear of being the next victim. Malek's words were incoherent due to the fierceness in which he spat them out. Any living thing he got close to was punched, kicked, or hurt with whatever object Malek happened to grab at the time. Malek knew the Presence had something to do with this, and he knew his daughter had played a part. How furious he was at the thought of his own daughter going against him! Even more than ever, he wished he had not missed that shot with the arrow!

Deciding that something needed to be done, Malek put his energy into finding the whereabouts of the Presence's chosen one, Wenzel. After much bribing, torture, and a little dark magic, Malek managed to find Wenzel, Trina, and William's location and decided to take matters into his own hands. He was going to stop the Presence once and for all! Wenzel was going to die!

It was a painstakingly long journey for Malek to climb up the snow-capped mountain alone. Without the help of the Presence, it was nearly impossible. Had Malek not been driven mad by hate, he would never have had the endurance to continue. The path Wenzel and his parents had taken was now covered over in deep snow, and the wind blew more fiercely than before. But Malek trudged on. His hatred was the only thing that kept him going. He finally reached the cave where he knew Wenzel was hiding with his parents. The sun had just begun to rise so Malek hid behind a boulder just outside the mouth of the cave. He waited for Wenzel to come out of the cave and fall into his trap!

While the others were still sleeping, Wenzel began to stir. He slept solidly for a few hours from pure fatigue, but now that the sun was coming up, he couldn't sleep. Not wanting to disturb the others, he exited the safety of the cave to get some fresh air. With so many thoughts racing around in his head, Wenzel was distracted and didn't take note of his surroundings. All of a sudden, and without hesitation, Malek took his opportunity and lunged forward ready to stab Wenzel with a dagger. But right as Malek was about to stab Wenzel, Kelam jumped out from the cave! Malek recognized him immediately! Enraged that he was still alive, Malek turned and tackled the creature to the ground. Kelam struggled against Malek's dominating strength knocking the dagger out of his hand.

Wenzel just stood frozen in shock. He couldn't believe he was standing staring at the man he'd been running from! The commotion awoke Trina and William, and they came dashing out of the cave to see what was happening. As they ran and grabbed Wenzel, they paused as they heard soft melodic music begin to play from under Kelam's shirt. It made all of them, including Malek, pause to listen more closely. It came from a locket. Malek looked as if he had seen a ghost! A mix of emotions engulfed him. Feeling deep anguish, despair, and hate, Malek grabbed the only destructive object in sight, a rock, and with all his force, smashed the musical locket around Kelam's neck in one swift blow. The creature gasped for air, unable to catch his breath! Malek, confused in a range of emotions, grabbed the creature's head, held it, and stared into its fading eyes. The song from the locket broke Malek's hatred into pain and sadness, losing his immortality. Wenzel, Trina, and William fearfully watched not knowing what to do or what was happening. The man of pure evil was holding the head of the son he had just murdered. As quickly as the wind blew, Malek became enraged one last time. He stood up from the lifeless creature and growled at the sky! "Will you never leave me!" He shouted to a distant painful memory.

Malek took the broken locket from around Kelam's neck and placed it over his heart, and died. His body instantly dissolved into dust. Like that, Malek was gone! In complete shock, Wenzel sank to the ground, staring at the dead body, the pile of ash, and the broken locket. *Is this a trick of dark magic?* he questioned.

Out of stress and exhaustion from his life over the past few months, Wenzel began to deeply weep. Trina knelt down next to him and held him as he wept. He had made a friend and watched him die in a day's time. Now, they were stranded on top of the mountain with no way of telling the others what had happened. War was on the verge of erupting, and it would be for nothing now! Malek was dead! The power he once had over the Land of Arar was over. Wenzel had to do something!

Without warning, a gust of wind picked up the ashes from the snow then knocked Wenzel over pushing Trina to the side. William ran to Trina making sure she was alright. The strength of the dust filled wind pinned Wenzel down! "Let me go!" Wenzel yelled out of frustration and helplessness. At that, the wind swirled down disappearing with a shriek of anguish into the barren snow. Wenzel sat up, confused and tired. He cried again. Then, from the mouth of the cave, blew a piece of paper. It glided through the wind until it landed at Wenzel's feet. He sat waiting for something else to happen, but nothing did. He cautiously picked up the paper surprised to see it was addressed to him. It read:

"My dear friend Wenzel,

I fear that my time on this mountain is coming to an early end. It is a shame that after all these years, I finally found a true friend only to have to leave you. So, I will give you this knowledge. The locket I wore around my neck belonged to my grandmother, Malek's mother. It contained the only good memory in Malek's life, the song she sang to him and his twin sister every night. It was his only weakness. The Presence says that I have her eyes.

The territory of Malek, Arar, has been recruiting its best, most gruesome fighters, merciless fighters. Victory is Arar's . . . or so it seems. I have been privileged to walk with the Presence of the Hill on many occasions. That is how I know all that I've told you. So, once again, I leave you with this . . . victory is not lost! The Hill has been secretly recruiting the finest and wisest warriors from allies around the world. Ships disguised as sea creatures have made nightly voyages, bringing in thousands of men at once. They are in the cover of the Secret Keepers of the Unfound Valley. I have enclosed a map. Guard it with your life, Wenzel. Arar must never find out! Once I am gone, you and your parents must move quickly and find the others. Tell them all that has occurred on this mountain. It will give them hope and perhaps an advantage. War is imminent. And Wenzel, thank you for your friendship. I know I am not pleasant to

look at, yet you never looked away when I talked to you.
Thank you and good-bye.
Kelam"

With his heart pounding in his chest, he hurriedly gave the letter to his parents then ran into the cave to gather together anything he thought could help them. With the letter tucked in Wenzel's pocket, they headed down the mountain towards Unfound Valley.

XXXII

The Secret Keepers

They had been traveling all day down and out of the South Mountains. The map was easy enough to follow. It was the terrain that was difficult. By night they had reached the Unfound Valley. If it hadn't been for Kelam's map, they would have never stumbled across it. Truly, it was hidden deep in the crevices on the edges of the South Mountains. On the map, Kelam wrote specific instructions to only cross the Unfound Valley during the day. If not, the Night Seekers would pursue them. Night Seekers were nasty four legged creatures with vulture-like heads and bodies of large dogs. They ate only freshly dead meat and harassed the nearly dead to death. They wait until the victim dies before they feast. From all that had happened to Wenzel, Trina, and William in the last couple of days, they were fatigued to the point of collapsing. The only thing that kept them going now, was being so close to telling the others what had happened. The confrontation with Malek had left them physically and emotionally scarred. The scent of death lingered on them, which made them even more vulnerable to the Night Seekers. The map showed that they were nearly at the Secret Keepers.

Squinting through the darkness, William spotted the enchanted forest across the valley. He quietly grabbed Wenzel's shoulder and pointed across the vast ravine. Being careful not to make much noise in fear of drawing attention to themselves, Trina nodded that she saw it too. It was just as Kelam described it on the map—a densely packed group of trees that not even the wind could get through.

What Wenzel wasn't sure of was how they were going to cross the Unfound Valley in the dark and get inside the Secret Keepers. Just then, as if his thoughts were heard, a wind out of nowhere swept up a pile of fallen sticks to reveal what looked like a grass covered door. It was hard to see in the dim moonlight, but Wenzel walked over to the door and opened it. Inside was a dirt tunnel with a set of clay stairs. It was just tall enough for them to stand inside, bent over slightly. Having no other safe choice, they entered, shutting the door securely behind them. In complete darkness they walked in silence around a curve.

There, they saw a faint light! It burned hope inside their weary hearts. As they got closer, they discovered a lantern lit path along an underground river. Pushed up to shore was an ancient-looking boat, exactly like the one Charlie, Wenzel, and Muriphany took not too long ago. In the boat, they used a long pole to push themselves down the river. The channel lasted about a mile until it ended at another shore full of boats. Hopeful they were almost to the

Secret Keepers' center, Wenzel jumped out of the boat and ran up the stairs forgetting to wait for Trina and William. The steps, just as Wenzel had hoped, indeed led right into the interior of the Secret Keepers! Before he could see anyone, a hand grabbed his face from behind, wrestling him to the ground. He was unable to speak or breathe. "Hush!" a voice said. "Be still, or you will die." Then he heard the beating of a drum echoing off the trees and realized it wasn't his heart. They were drums, deep bass drums, that would have carried for miles if not surrounded by the dense forest.

The stranger lifted his hand off Wenzel's face, and Wenzel gasped for air. "Hush!" The voice said again, still not allowing Wenzel to see, but this time the voice sounded familiar. "I know who you are, and you've chosen a peculiar timing of your arrival. We thought you were one of them," the voice said concerned. "We fear our location has been jeopardized. We are no longer safe and have sent the signal that we are moving. You've come just in time." At that very moment, Trina and William emerged from the tunnel. Wenzel ran and stood in front of them guarding them against the same welcome he had endured.

"They are with me!" Wenzel spoke authoritatively. "We have news to share. Take us to who is in charge!" As he was speaking, his eyes adjusted enough to recognize the Wyse of the Lonely Manor! Quickly, Wenzel ran up to him wanting to hug him but resisted. "Is it still safe? The book?" He blurted out.

"Yes. Let me take you to the Wyse of the Hill. She is anxious to speak to you as well," the Wyse of the Lonely Manor replied seriously. In urgency, Trina, William, and Wenzel hurried after the Wyse of the Lonely Manor.

All around them was commotion. Everyone was in a hurry packing up their tents, weapons, and food supplies. Pack animals were lined up and being loaded. The faint moonlight cast an eery unsettling glow among the allies of the Hill. Fear and worry seemed to surround them. Finally, they reached the Wyse of the Hill. As they approached, she stopped speaking to a commander and spun around as if expecting them to arrive at that very moment. She handed over the maps she had been discussing with the commander to the Wyse of the Lonely Manor, then hurriedly walked to Wenzel, grabbing both his shoulders and lowering her eyes to his. "What has happened? You must tell me at once!" She spoke with such authority and seriousness that Wenzel and his parents explained their journey to the South Mountains, their encounter with Kelam, and the death of Malek, without hesitation. Shock and surprise filled her face as she listened. "Does anyone else know of this?" she demanded.

"No, just you. We haven't said a word to anyone else," William reassured.

With a whispered voice, the Wyse of the Hill said, "We have a traitor among us. Someone has been feeding information to Malek and his creatures. We are not safe here. I feel we will soon be under attack!"

"Who do you think it could be?" Trina questioned.

"We are not sure. That is why no one must know about what you have just spoken," the Wyse said, as she looked around suspiciously. "You better meet up with Charlie and Muriphany. They will be relieved to see you," she said, then quickly walked away.

Trina squeezed Wenzel's hand and said, "It will be okay. The Presence will guide us through this. He always has." The words of his mother soothed him as he gazed at his parents, but hearing Muriphany's name spoken by the Wyse put knots in his stomach. He knew who she was, and about her brother. Was she the one leaking information? Wenzel wasn't too sure. He needed to see her and talk to her privately.

Seeing the anguish on Wenzel's face, William put a reassuring hand on Wenzel's shoulder and said, "Go talk to her. We don't have much time." At that, Wenzel hugged his parents and set off to find Charlie and Muriphany. It seemed like he would never find them as he walked around and through the crowds of bustling people. A few times Wenzel nearly fell over something or tripped someone else. Then, just as he was standing up from a near encounter, Wenzel turned around only to come face-to-face with a sack of supplies. The force of the hit brought him to the ground.

"I'm so sorry!" a friendly voice shouted. Before Wenzel could respond, hands grabbed him and pulled him to his feet. There standing before him was a tired, dirty, and cheerful-looking Charlie. "You are here!" Charlie shouted! "I was wondering where you had gone! I got swept up with Ren leaving the island and didn't notice you weren't with us. Then I couldn't find you or Muriphany, but when we finally got to the Secret Keepers, Muriphany was already here. She was like a hero or something, saving all those people from Malek's Killing Grounds . . . " Charlie ranted on so quickly that Wenzel had a hard time keeping up.

"Wait!" Wenzel interrupted. "Where is Muriphany now?"

"She's over there. Behind you," he said pointing behind Wenzel's shoulder.

Wenzel gazed in that direction to see Muriphany carrying a heavy sack of equipment to load onto a mule. For the first time since they met, Wenzel saw her for her strength and determination. Knowing now about her past and what she had chosen to do, gave him a huge sense of respect and admiration for her. He was almost too nervous to approach her and speak. Gaining the courage, Wenzel walked over to Muriphany and helped tie the sack to the mule.

Without much tact, Wenzel looked at her and said, "We need to talk privately, immediately."

Wenzel spent the next hour telling Muriphany everything he had learned from her half-brother, Kelam, about the locket, and her father's past. Tears rolled down her cheeks as she grieved the loss of the brother she had never known. Muriphany told him about her near death experience with her father and about how the Presence led her to the Killing Grounds. Wenzel was so touched by her experiences and the choice to follow the Presence that he was certain she wasn't the traitor leaking information to the enemies. He knew he had to tell her about her father's death.

As Muriphany listened, grief overtook her, and she collapsed to the ground in uncontrollable sobbing. Her grief was for the father she never had in Malek, the loss of a dear brother who was rejected, and all the hurt that had come because of her father's past. Wenzel knelt down next to his friend and embraced her in his arms. Muriphany's sobbing calmed and she embraced him back. "We can't stay here. It's not safe. Even if my father is gone, there are others who believe just as he did. They will take his place. Arar must be destroyed," Muriphany explained solemnly. At that very moment, war horns sounded! They were under attack!

XXXIII

The Battle

Their hearts raced with adrenaline as Muriphany and Wenzel heard the first blare of the war horns! "It's happening! They are coming!" Muriphany shouted as she jumped to her feet. "Get weapons and be ready just as we have practiced!" She shouted to everyone around her with authority. To Wenzel's surprise, the people around her did exactly as they were told and were beginning to get into formation. Some even began building tall wooden catapults. Apparently, Wenzel had missed a lot while he was in the South Mountains. Suddenly, Charlie ran up to Wenzel handing him a sword. Trina and William joined them, armed and ready to fight. They had an advantage of knowledge, but how to use it was the question. Before Wenzel could take a step forward, out of nowhere the Wyse of the Hill spun him around.

"Run for the tunnel! Take Charlie and your parents and get out of here!" she shouted.

"What about Muriphany?" Wenzel replied, but the Wyse was gone before he could finish his question. Knowing that time was limited, Wenzel grabbed ahold of Charlie's sleeve and shouted to his parents to follow. The moon was still dim, and running through the chaos was unsettling and difficult. Suddenly, as if the earth was angry, the ground beneath them began to shake terribly. Each shake was stronger and louder than the previous time. Just as they reached the entrance to the tunnel, the strong, secure, never faulting Secret Keepers began to fall! Pound, shake, and down they went! The foursome stood in absolute astonishment as they witnessed the enchanted, stronghold trees fall to the earth.

Through the fallen barrier came Malek's men and creatures riding Earth Pounders! Enormous rhinoceros type animals, these beasts were enormous with the body structure of a rhinoceros which stood taller than houses. Each of their four legs was as thick as three full-grown oak trees, and at the end of each leg was a solid square hoof. The Allies watched in horror as the Earth Pounders forced their way through the fallen Secret Keepers. As each Earth Pounder stepped in unison, the force of their combined steps caused enough vibration through the ground to knock over more enchanted trees. It was nearly impossible for Wenzel, Charlie, Trina, and William to walk as the Earth Pounder's hooves hit the ground.

Just before the foursome dove into the tunnel, from the night sky, they heard flapping. Wenzel and Charlie glanced at each other with smiles. They knew that the dragons had arrived to help! Cheers from the allies erupted as the dragons flew over Malek's men, torching everything in their paths. Shrieks and cries of fear exploded from the enemies. Their enemies had not expected this!

Carefully, Charlie, Wenzel, Trina, and William walked down the stairs of the underground tunnel. Now that the Earth Pounders were no longer marching in unison, they were able to walk quickly down the stairs with only bits of dirt and stone falling from the tunnel ceiling. Upon reaching the river, to their shock, almost all the boats were gone! There were only a few left. Wenzel, William, and Trina looked about suspiciously at the lack of boats. "What's up, guys? Shouldn't we just hop in a boat and get out of here?" Charlie asked innocently.

"You don't understand. All the boats were at this end of the tunnel when we arrived. Now, it's as if a bunch of people have fled from the battle," Wenzel said grimly.

"Who would flee? All the people in the Secret Keepers came to fight Malek and his followers," William said. Before anyone could say anything else, they heard voices further down the tunnel. The foursome huddled together and sank back into the shadows to hide from whomever was approaching. From the darkness, they saw a boat coming down the tunnel. It was full of people. As it got closer, Wenzel recognized the Wyse of the Lonely Manor standing in the front of the boat holding Charlie's leather bound, clock book! But before he could be relieved at the sight of the book, the foursome spotted, sitting behind the Wyse of the Lonely Manor, some of the ugliest, most gruesome creatures they had ever seen! He was leading Malek's men right to the center of the Secret Keepers! HE was the traitor! And he was using the book to do it.

Instinctively, William, Trina, Wenzel, and Charlie got into position to ambush the boat. From the corner of his eye, Charlie spotted a long beam supporting the ceiling from collapsing. If he timed it correctly, he could collapse the ceiling over the boat as it came close to the stairs. He stood perfectly still watching and waiting for the precise moment to arrive. His heart beat slowly in his chest as the boat inched closer and closer. Time stood still. Charlie drew in a deep breath, and then with all his might jumped forward using the momentum of his body to dislodge the support beam. Before the Wyse knew what was happening, the ceiling above them collapsed, capsizing the boat. The weight of the soil and rocks from the ceiling pinned some of Malek's men under water.

William, Trina, and Wenzel took Charlie's distraction as an opportunity to finish off those who were trying to get out of the river. Wenzel saw the Wyse of the Lonely Manor frantically looking around for the book as he splashed around the water in a panic. Wenzel grabbed his sword tightly in two hands and went charging at the Wyse. Instead of stabbing him, Wenzel hit the Wyse on the head with the butt end of the sword. Before his unconscious body could slip beneath the water, William came from behind and grabbed the Wyse dragging him out. Breathing heavily from exertion, the foursome gathered around the Wyse of the Lonely Manor looking down at him. He was still breathing. Charlie took rope from one of the boats still left and threw it to William.

Together, they bound their prisoner's hands and feet and gagged his mouth.

"There will be others," Trina said breaking the silence.

"He must have taken the boats to the other side for Malek's men and creatures to use," William added.

"Then we must move faster than them. Get in the boat!" Wenzel demanded. The others grabbed their weapons and threw them into a remaining boat. They each grabbed hold of the Wyse of the Lonely Manor and tossed him, not so gently, into the boat. He was still unconscious. By now, the capsized boat had sunk to the bottom and the ceiling had finished dropping dirt and rocks. They quickly pushed off the side of the river and began making their way down the tunnel.

"What's the plan?" Charlie asked feeling anxious.

"We will see when we get to the other end," William answered solemnly.

"Oh, by the way! Look what I grabbed!" Charlie exclaimed as he pulled the book from under his shirt. He had tucked it into his belt soon after the ceiling collapsed on the enemies.

"Put it away! It's not safe!" Wenzel shouted, surprising himself by his abrupt reaction. "Sorry, I'm relieved you've got it. We must not let it out of our hands. We can't trust anyone now," he said trailing off.

"The good news is that we have the book and have the advantage of knowing that Malek is dead. Perhaps we have a chance of invading Arar successfully," Trina said, trying to lift the spirits of the four.

"What?!?!" Charlie shouted, not knowing Malek was dead. But before the others could respond, they reached the end of the tunnel.

"Hush!" Wenzel whispered, bringing his finger to his lips. Together the four sat in silence, listening for signs of more enemies. The missing boats were still tied up at this end of the tunnel which meant their prisoner had been the first boat to try to enter the interior of the Secret Keepers. That was good news! William elbowed Charlie and pointed to another beam holding up the ceiling. Then he pointed to the other side of the staircase to see more beams. If they ordered it correctly, the four of them, along with their prisoner, could collapse the tunnel and escape unharmed.

"First strap your weapons on," Wenzel whispered, "Then Mom and Dad, take our prisoner up the stairs while Charlie and I collapse the tunnel." That had been the first time he called his parents "Mom" and "Dad." Oh! How he wished he could have savored the moment, but there wasn't time. Trina and William with eyes rimmed with tears, grabbed ahold of their prisoner and made their way towards the stairs. They, too, understood that now was not the time for sentiment.

XXXIV

Muriphany and Her Dragons

The battle horns blared, and the Earth Pounders shook the ground. Muriphany looked about, impressed at the courage of those who continued to stand in their formations despite every reason to run in fear. Brave men and women stood unwaveringly in the face of evil. Suddenly, her tattoo began to burn hot! The dragons were coming! But her tattoo did something it never did before! It began to hum. It was a soft melodic tune she had never heard, but it was beautiful and soothing. The dragons seemed to respond to it as they turned to her direction as soon as the tattoo hummed. Fire poured out of their nostrils as they flew over the Earth Pounders on their way to Muriphany. Their strength and beauty sent shivers down her spine as she watched them effortlessly take down the enemy.

Lifting her sword high in the air, she shouted, "Charge!" Immediately the allies of the Hill charged forward in astonishing numbers and strength. Each encounter with the enemy was met with a successful blow. They were winning! It seemed like only minutes had passed as the Allies of the Hill destroyed the enemy. Malek's followers were confused and began running around in fear and chaos. Some fled out of the Secret Keepers and into the traps of the Night Seekers. The Night Seekers' excited howls could be heard as they circled the enchanted forest, drawn to it by the smell of fresh death.

The sun's beams slowly began to pierce through the darkness. As smoke billowed up from burnt trees and carcasses, the Allies began to assess their victory. Relief filled their hearts as friends and loved ones were reunited. Not one of Malek's men remained. The dragons landed gracefully for a much-needed rest, and Muriphany ordered a group of men to bring water for the dragons to drink. Her heart felt full looking at the magnificent beasts. She felt a new deeper connection with them. Her father wanted her to use these dragons to destroy the Hill, but she had changed her fate and used them for good. Tears of joy and relief rolled down her cheeks as she hugged the neck of one of her new friends.

XXXV

The Tail of the Beast

Following Trina and William's lead, Charlie and Wenzel stayed closely behind. Not knowing exactly what to do with the Wyse of the Lonely Manor, they left him tied up to a tree outside what remained of the Secret Keepers. They figured that being tormented by the Night Seekers was the least of his self-earned punishments. If they returned from Arar, they would make sure he was fairly tried before the Council of the Wyse. But for now, they just hoped they would make it to Arar unseen.

Even though many years had passed, Trina and William, unfortunately, were very familiar with the way to Arar. As they got closer and closer to its borders, everything around them began to lose life. The smell of rotting flesh and decay filled the air. Charlie held back from being sick as they continued closer. The trees were black with scale insects that slowly suffocated trees, making them look as if they were being tortured. Even the rocks looked sickly. The ground around them seemed to ooze and puss sulfuric acid. Noticing the disgusted looks on Charlie and Wenzel's faces, William paused and said, "Don't worry. We are just about there. The good news is that it doesn't smell worse than it does now." Then he continued on. Trina chuckled to herself as she followed.

"How can you laugh? The smell is burning my eyes!" Charlie said frantically.

Trina and William glanced at each other and smirked again. Trying not to gag from the smell, Wenzel added, "Quite the sense of humor you two have! We are suffering, and you go on as if we were wimps."

Finally, William threw back a little pouch, hitting Wenzel in the chest. "Rub some under your nose. It stops the smell," William said with another smirk. As quickly as they could open the pouch, they dipped their fingers in some sort of oil and herb mixture and then even more quickly rubbed it under their noses. Instantly, they were relieved from the smell.

"What is this stuff!" Charlie exclaimed.

"Oh, it's just a little something we invented years ago when we were holding secret meetings out in these woods around Arar. In Arar, it looks just as ugly, but it smells less," Trina explained.

"Well, thanks for finally sharing some!" Wenzel said, part jokingly and partly offended. Trina just giggled in response.

"Wait! I hear something!" William alerted the others. All four of them stood perfectly still, earnestly listening to what was coming. Up until now, they had not crossed paths with anyone else. Unexpectedly, something under Wenzel's jacket began to burn! He quickly reached into his inside pocket, grabbing whatever was burning him, and he threw it to the ground. It was Kelam's letter! And it was glowing bright red! The other three quickly turned their attention towards the letter as well. Charlie had no idea what was going on but felt that it was best to ask questions later. Gazing at the glowing note, Wenzel noticed that the words began to change. The black ink began to expand and run into each other until there was just a large black ink blot in the center of the glowing hot paper. Suddenly, the letter imploded into the ink blot making a large popping noise. The four-some dove for cover, fearing it was a bomb. When nothing happened, Wenzel looked back over to where the letter had been, only to see dark smoke coming from it. He jumped back to his feet and ran over to it. In its place was a large black gem, the size of Wenzel's fist! Not afraid, Wenzel grabbed it off the ground and began to exam it.

"It can't be!" exclaimed William, running up to Wenzel and nearly snatching it out of his hand.

"We have only heard whispers of this, rumors. To think that it is real and right in front of us is truly a miracle!" Trina said, astonished.

"What is it?" Charlie said unsure of the magnitude of the event.

"The Stone of Arar," Wenzel whispered as he stared at it. "The Wyse of the Hill told me a story about it. It was always thought to be a myth, a legend at best. She said that when the Hill was founded by our forefather, Isaac, they entered the mouth of the Beast, the mountain formation that completely encircles the Hill. Malek was always jealous and hated the fact that he did not enter it with Isaac.

The story goes that one day, Malek, after establishing his own colony in Arar, snuck out to attack the beast. He had decided to climb up its tail and steal one of its spikes. After hours of treacherous climbing, and nearly falling to his death, Malek finally reached the tail of the Beast. Black gems studded the tail spikes of the Beast, and Malek wanted to steal one so that he could say he conquered it. But as he chipped at the Beast's tail trying to loosen a gem, the Presence himself stood before Malek. At first, it is said, Malek was scared at being caught, but then he became angrier than ever before. He thought he deserved this gem! He felt he worked just as hard as Isaac had! Hatred and jealousy filled his entire being. At the very same moment, the black gem loosened into his hand. It was large and with jagged edges. Malek lurched forward attempting to stab the Presence in anger.

But of course, the Presence vanished, and Malek tripped, stabbing his own leg with the gem. Blood oozed over the gem, and Malek screamed out in pain and deep anger. That night his hatred immortalized him, and the stone became the folklore of the land of Arar."

"Yes, you are correct," Trina said solemnly with a dazed look of memory on her face.

"He used to threaten us, saying its power would kill us if we became loyal to anyone other than him," William added.

"But no one ever saw it," Trina said taking a step closer to it.

Lifting the gem up in the air, Wenzel said, "And now the Presence gave it to us." They all stood staring at it for a moment.

Then Charlie, feeling a little out of the loop, chimed in, "Soooo, what do we do with it?"

"I don't know," Wenzel said disappointingly, dropping his arm to his side, looking down at it in his hand.

"I do!" chimed in a fifth voice. All at once, the foursome spun around with swords drawn! Wenzel slipped the gem into his pocket and grabbed his sword with both hands.

To their complete shock, Muriphany stood in front of them with her arms up in surrender. "Sorry, I didn't mean to startle you. I thought you heard me coming," she said apologetically.

Charlie immediately lowered his sword as did Wenzel, but Trina and William stayed with weapons drawn. "Let me explain," Muriphany went on, "I am the only other person who has seen the Stone of Arar. In my training to destroy the Hill, my father often showed it to me and explained its power. It is infused with dark and evil spells."

"Can it be destroyed?" Wenzel asked as he motioned his parents to lower their weapons.

"Yes, but it's a little complicated," Muriphany said.

"We can handle complicated," Trina said, suggesting Muriphany better continue.

"My father made it that in order for the Stone of Arar to be destroyed, and ultimately Arar, it must be laid on the dragon's eye. When it is on the dragon's eye, another dragon will breathe its fire on it, and it will be incinerated. Furthermore, this has to take place at the very spot at which it was stolen," Muriphany said, looking forlorn.

"What dragon will let us lay the Stone of Arar on its eye? That's impossible," Charlie sputtered out in exasperation, feeling out of the loop with all this new information about Muriphany.

Seeing deep into Muriphany's underlying tone, Wenzel replied worriedly, "No, it's not. It's as simple as asking for Muriphany's permission."

Charlie's eyes widened as he remembered her dragon tattoo with the large black eye. He had remembered thinking the eye was disproportionally large for the dragon as they laid the stones on her back, so many days ago. Muriphany stood thinking as a tear trickled down her cheek. "I give you my permission. It must be done," she said, definitively.

Trina and William exchanged confused glances before four other dragons arrived to take them to the Beast's tail. As Muriphany was getting the dragons ready to have passengers, Wenzel took Trina and William aside and explained the whole thing to them. Trina and William kept glancing over at Muriphany as they listened to the wild tale of what the trio had been through.

Muriphany, feeling a bit shy and exposed, asked, "Are you ready to go? The dragons are prepared."

"Yeah, and I'm getting hungry," Charlie said not realizing the inappropriate timing of his comment. It made Muriphany laugh subtly for the first time in a long time.

Taking that as a cue to get moving, Wenzel headed towards a dragon and hopped on. Trina and William walked arm-in-arm over to Muriphany, and, without saying a word, grabbed her in an embrace between the two of them. No words were needed. She knew their gratitude. Once everyone was seated on a dragon. Muriphany's tattoo hummed and the dragons took off.

If it had not been for the task at hand, the flight to the Beast's tail would have been magnificent. The beauty of the South Mountains, the sea, and the Beast itself, was simply astonishing! But this flight was solemn. With the Stone of Arar in his pocket, Wenzel kept his eyes straight ahead on the Beast's tail, wondering how the Presence was going to come through.

XXXVI

Destruction

The Beast's tail was wide enough for the dragons to land and for the five of them to dismount. There was no joyous chatter as they stood in one of the most beautiful places of all time. The tail of the Beast overlooked the South Mountains and the sparkling waters of the sea. Instead, they walked to the only place that looked bare. Wenzel took the Stone of Arar out of his pocket and placed it gently in the bare spot. To his dismay, it was a perfect fit. Without a word, Muriphany walked over to Wenzel and laid down on her stomach, raising the back of her shirt just enough for the eye of the dragon on her tattoo to be seen. Wenzel, with tears in his eyes, placed the Stone of Arar on her back. It was a perfect fit. Then Wenzel stood up and stepped back, taking a place next to his parents and Charlie. At that same moment, the tattoo began to glow and hum deeply. All but one dragon lowered their heads and bowed. The fifth dragon slowly walked towards Muriphany, cocked its neck back preparing the inferno inside, and then released the flame with a roar over the Stone of Arar!

The foursome gasped in shock as the flame engulfed Muriphany! Wenzel buried his head in his father's chest, and Charlie spun around, looking away, not wanting to see Muriphany die. The dragon breathed fire for what seemed an eternity. Wenzel began to weep heavily at the thought of not thinking to say goodbye. He had just expected the Presence to step in and protect her. Trina shielded her face from the heat, and William looked away, not knowing if destroying the Stone of Arar was worth it.

Finally, the dragon ceased his fire-breathing. The foursome remained looking away in fear of seeing Muriphany's body scorched to a crisp. Then breaking the silence, Muriphany said, "Did it work?" Wenzel, Charlie, Trina, and William exclaimed in excitement and relief as they ran towards her to see if she was harmed! To their amazement, the Stone of Arar was completely destroyed. Only charred, smoking dust remained on Muriphany's back. Muriphany herself was completely un-scorched.

"Impossible!" Trina said examining Muriphany's skin.

"How did you not get hurt?" William asked suspiciously.

"You should be dead!" Charlie stated.

"I'm glad you are unharmed, but I don't understand how," added Wenzel.

"I wasn't sure if it was a dream or if it really happened. So I didn't want to depend on it. When we were living at the Lonely Manor, and you and Charlie brought me to Professor Longtree for help, I was unconscious from the curse my father had placed on me and that necklace. As Professor Longtree worked on me, I had a dream that she was placing something over me, it lifted off my father's control and dark powers. Every time she rubbed on an ointment, I felt as if she was coating me in a protection of some sort. I guess her work that night was more permanent than any of us expected," Muriphany said, sitting up and hugging her legs.

Charlie and Wenzel laid a sympathetic and grateful hand on each of her shoulders, but before any of the five of them could say another word, the ground beneath them began to shake and quiver! "Earthquake!" William shouted as each of them struggled to brace themselves. Then the mountain beneath them began to rise higher and higher as if the Beast itself had awoken.

Wedged between two boulders and holding onto a tree branch, Charlie looked out and saw that in fact, the mountain had awoken! The mountain that was shaped like a beast that curled itself around the Hill, where Wenzel once lived, was now walking around like a giant dragon ready to devour anything in its sight. They began to sway to and fro, as the tail of the beast moved back and forth.

"Where are we going?" shouted Wenzel.

"I think I am going to be sick," Charlie said, feeling nauseous.

"We are headed towards Arar!" Trina exclaimed, pointing out the location to William.

The beast was indeed going towards Arar and nothing could stop it. Its eyes glowed and steam billowed from its nostrils. A low growl escaped its mouth as it swaggered slowly towards Arar. Each step crushed trees and made craters in the earth. Animals for miles around ran in the opposite direction of the Beast in fear of being devoured. The creature looked from side-to-side before pointing its snout up to the sky letting out a dreadful howl.

"We are going to die!" Charlie cried out. He struggled to keep his grip on the branch, in fear of falling off the Beast.

From all parts of the sky, dark storm clouds raced in, covering the land below in great darkness. The closer the Beast got to Arar, the more agitated it became with growls and howls. Its tail rested on the ground just long enough to give them all a chance to jump off. Landing in a rough heap, the five quickly sat up and looked towards Arar as the Beast entered in. With its enormous size, it began to swallow up everything and everyone in its path. Screams and shouts could be heard, followed by silence.

As the Beast ate, it grew larger and larger until it looked as if it were about to burst, sending shards of rocks and gems shooting out. But right as it was about to explode, a great light began to glow within its center. The light grew brighter and brighter until blinding beams shot out every crack and crevice of the creature. It flashed in an intense pulse knocking down every tree and person within close range. The five fell to the ground as the warm light raced over them. They shielded their eyes from its intensity. Then, there was silence.

As Muriphany opened her eyes, she was speechless. Sitting in the place of Arar was the most beautiful gem-covered mountain she had ever seen! It was pure white stone speckled with the gems of the Beast. Every ugly thing that once had surrounded Arar was now replaced with magnificent stone pillars and rock towers. The land sparkled with decadence and erased the memory from the land of the evil that dwelled there for so long.

Muriphany stood up to better take in the view. As she took a step forward, a warmth filled her body and her tattoo began to hum deeply, calling to her dragons. Within seconds, the dragons arrived, each one landing on a stone pillar or rock tower. The combination of the two made Muriphany weak at the knees.

Charlie quickly grabbed the book and opened it, hoping to find some information about what he was seeing. The first page read: Queen Muriphany of the Land of the Dragons. Without continuing, he looked up to see each dragon bowing down to her. Then, one dragon walked towards her and placed a gem covered white crown on her head. With tears in her eyes, she turned to the other four and mouthed the words, "Thank you."

Dropping all propriety, Wenzel ran up to her and grabbed her in his arms holding her tightly. She embraced him back, letting the tears roll down her cheeks. Trina and William joined in hugging Muriphany. They too were relieved that Arar and Malek had finally been destroyed! Charlie put the book back in his belt and raced up to them, nearly knocking them over as he joined in.

XXXVII

Celebration

It seemed as if it had been a different lifetime the last Charlie and Wenzel sat in the house of the Wyse of the Hill. Though only months had passed, Charlie and Wenzel had become men. In fact, they were gathered on the Isle of the Wyse to celebrate the wedding of Wenzel and Muriphany. Trina and William Bennington fussed over Wenzel, making sure his wedding clothes were just right. Aunt Trudy and Uncle Lucas shed tears at the happy reunion of their family. Charlie watched as Trina covered Wenzel's face in a thousand kisses while saying something through her sobs of joy. Feeling a little awkward about being in the room during this intimate family moment, Charlie slipped out, careful not to wrinkle his clothes. Wenzel had asked Charlie to be his best man. Charlie was more than honored to accept now that he was a young man of 13. Somehow during the crazy adventure, he had missed his birthday.

He made his way down the beautiful corridor remembering back to when he had last been there. The sun was shining brightly, and the birds were singing songs of joy as if they knew what today was. Coming up to a door cracked open, Charlie paused as a motion behind it caught his eye. He stepped closer and peeked in, only to see Muriphany standing before a full-length mirror in a pure white gown! The sight of her took his breath away. Her wedding gown had long sleeves and a high neck. The backless dress revealed her dragon tattoo perfectly which drew your eye down to the long, lace train which reached a few feet behind her. A white veil lay over her dark brown hair and tranquil face. The lace of the veil mimicked the lace of her gown. Charlie caught himself from not breathing, swallowed hard, and then gathered the courage to gently knock on the door. "It's me, Charlie. Can I come in?" he gently asked.

"Yes, please," Muriphany replied. Charlie entered and Muriphany turned toward him as she held a bouquet of red roses. A gentle joyful smile lit up her face under the veil as Charlie walked up to her.

"Wow! You look amazing, Muriphany! I . . . I . . . mean Queen Muriphany," Charlie stuttered sheepishly.

Taking one hand and putting it on Charlie's shoulder she said, "Don't be silly. You are my dear friend. Call me Muriphany."

Relieved, Charlie continued, "Are you ready? The ceremony begins any minute."

Gazing down at her bouquet, a look of deep sadness crossed her face. Startled Charlie jumped in, "What is it?"

Taking a breath, she said, "I wish I had parents to be here for this day."

"Well, I don't know about parents, but how about really good friends," said a voice coming in through the door. Both Muriphany and Charlie quickly turned their heads towards the door. It was Ren and his twin brother Mr. Ignas, followed by the fifteen other traitors of Malek, as well as the thirty people she rescued from the Killing Grounds. "We wouldn't miss this day for the world!" Ren exclaimed with a grin.

The wedding ceremony of Queen Muriphany and Wenzel was the most beautiful and perfect ceremony Charlie had ever seen. Their love for each other and deep commitment to one another was magnified and celebrated. When they were pronounced husband and wife, the entire cathedral erupted in cheers as flower petals showered down from the ceiling.

The reception was full of the most delicious foods and drinks Charlie had ever tasted! Fancy platters of meats, cheeses, fruits, nuts, and roasted vegetables lined the tables of the enormous hall. The dessert table was its very own masterpiece. Wenzel and Queen Muriphany's ten-tier wedding cake decorated with frosted dragons took center place. Around it were pies, tarts, and candies of the greatest assortment.

The entire hall was filled with joyous laughter and dancing. Toast after toast went out to the newly-married friends. There was so much relief and cause for celebration. Charlie, after taking another bite of dessert, plopped down onto a cushioned chair and just took it all in. He smiled and chuckled to himself as he looked about reminiscing on recent events.

The Wyse of the Lonely Manor had been tried by the council of the Wyse and sentenced to life as a slave in a faraway land. Never again would he step foot in the land of the Presence. The villagers of the Hill had all begun to resettle into the newly expanded Hill now that the Beast was no longer needed there. The land of the dragons was growing as baby dragons began to hatch. Ren and Mr. Ignas became the new keepers of the Lonely Manor, but they decided to rename it since it was no longer a lonely place. They felt that Longtree Manor was much more fitting. Everything had seemed to fall perfectly into place. All of Malek's followers were instantly destroyed when the light from the beast shot out across the land. Peace and order had been restored to the land of the Presence. Love won!

Charlie picked up another piece of dessert and was about to stuff the whole thing in his mouth when a firm hand grabbed onto his shoulder. At first, Charlie was startled, but then, as he turned around, he knew it was time. It was time for him to return back to his world. During his time with Wenzel, he never stopped to think about how he would return or when. He didn't want to. Sadness began to overwhelm him, but when he looked at the Presence holding his shoulder, he knew that he was going to be just fine. Taking one last glance around the hall, Charlie watched as the people in the room continued their joyous celebrating. He watched as Muriphany and Wenzel held hands and danced amongst their friends.

Knowing it was time, Charlie put down his plate and followed the Presence out of the hall. They walked down the now dark corridor since it was well into the middle of the night. The corridor became darker and darker as they walked, and the further they walked, the harder it was for Charlie to see the Presence in front of him. He continued walking anyway until his face hit a wall with a thud! "Ouch!" exclaimed Charlie. He began to feel the wall in front of him hoping to find the Presence standing near, but instead, he felt a familiar door knob. He slowly turned the knob and pushed it open.

He peered out. He was back inside Auntie Phranzie and Uncle Ralph's house! Relief and sadness filled him. *How will I ever be the same after that?* He thought to himself. Realizing he was still in the forbidden room, he heard footsteps coming closer and immediately shut the secret door. Charlie began to nervously sweat. He had no idea how he was going to sneak out.

To his relief, Uncle Ralph entered the clock room and shut off the light he had left on. Upon exiting the room, he left the door surprisingly open. Charlie waited for many minutes until he was certain his uncle was out of sight. Quickly and quietly, Charlie opened the secret door and crawled out from under the desk as fast as possible. With his eyes still adjusting to the days natural light, he scurried out of the room, past the bathroom just as Uncle Ralph was coming out.

"Have to use the toilet, as well?" Uncle Ralph rhetorically questioned as he shuffled past Charlie and back to his room. Charlie just nodded as he went by. When he was sure that Uncle Ralph was gone, Charlie raced up the ladder to the attic room and threw himself on the bed. Tears poured out as he curled himself in a ball not wanting to be back but wanting to stay with Wenzel and Muriphany.

In that moment, Charlie remembered the book! Desperately, he searched his belt where he had made a habit of keeping it. It wasn't there! Charlie's heart sank further at the thought of losing that, too. As Charlie started to put his head in his hands to sob, something caught his eye. Across the room, sitting on an old dresser was a gold-bound book he had not noticed before. Nearly jumping out of his skin, he raced over to it grabbing it with both hands to see. And there on the front cover were Muriphany's dragons and the title read, "Charlie, The Dragon Trainer."

Married to G. P. Bassett and the mother of two, A. Lynn Bassett holds a bachelor's degree in psychology with a focus on anthropology. Her love of other cultures, people, and places led to her extensive travels in Asia.

Bilingual in Mandarin and English, Bassett eagerly seeks out new adventures and experiences that inspire her stories. On any given day, she's either enjoying a good book with a hot cup of tea or hiking up the nearest mountain with her family.

Made in the USA
Columbia, SC
20 March 2018